Chloe's **HOPE**

Deb Quinlan

authorHOUSE®

AuthorHouse™
1663 Liberty Drive
Bloomington, IN 47403
www.authorhouse.com
Phone: 1 (800) 839-8640

Published by AuthorHouse   07/31/2015

ISBN: 978-1-5049-1932-6 (sc)
ISBN: 978-1-5049-1931-9 (e)

Library of Congress Control Number: 2015910139

Print information available on the last page.

Any people depicted in stock imagery provided by Thinkstock are
models, and such images are being used for illustrative purposes only.
Certain stock imagery © Thinkstock.

This book is printed on acid-free paper.

Contents

Chapter 1

Chloe groaned as she tried to grasp the baby in her dream. It was a repeat dream that was fading even as she reached through the haze for the baby with the familiar pain squeezing her heart. As she was about to touch it, the baby drifted away into a beautiful sunset. She awoke feeling the same heavy sadness and tears as always, as well as the confusion regarding the sunset in the dream. For such a sad dream, it should be in black and white or something more attuned to her loss.

After lying for several minutes, taking deep breaths and letting go of the dream, the only consolation was that the dreams were coming less frequently. She supposed that was normal since a little over a year had passed since the accident. It could also be recurring at this time because she was ready, or at least she thought she was, to pursue the idea of adoption. It is adoption as a single parent.

Sighing deeply, she sat up and forced her feet onto the floor, wiggling her toes as the dream remnants finally disappeared. She had gotten better about getting out of bed like a normal person, even though each time she had the dream, it set her back just a bit.

Anger toward God was still in her heart and mind even though she believed he was still active in her life. After all, she was still alive, even though struggling with not being able to have a child still tortured her. She had not been to church since the accident. Even though she had been tempted recently to go, it was not enough to bring her through the church doors.

Today was a big day for her. She appreciated her friend who was a child care company owner that always admired how well she took care of family member children and children of friends. She applied for a childcare position which the friend was happy about. She was looking forward to be taking care of an eight year old girl the friend requested of her. It would be part time and only for a couple of months or less. Her goal was to get more experience with a child, one on one, and not a child that is a blood relative. Even though she changed the diapers of nieces and nephews and spends a lot of time with them as they grow up, to have the responsibility of one of her own was a little daunting. It was especially daunting knowing she'd be raising the child alone, someone else's child. A familiar sadness seeped in at the thought of never having her own child snuggled beneath her heart as it grew for nine months. Thoughts of her ex-fiancé Andrew tried to overtake her mind and she pushed them away.

After taking a shower and having breakfast, she gathered her wits together and headed out the door. Ten minutes later she was sitting in front of Mr. Kurt Simpson's home not too far from her Connecticut home. Kurt was an accountant who lost his wife to cancer two years ago. His eight-year-old daughter needed after school care with the possibility of watching her a few nights and a Saturday here and there as well.

Heart racing, she pulled her hands off the steering wheel. Taking in deep breaths, she chided herself, whispering, "Chloe Wheeler, get a hold of yourself."

The front door of the two story ranch house opened and she saw the little girl step out onto the porch. Chloe swallowed and forced her shaking hands to relax as she looked at herself in the rearview mirror, fixing imaginary out of place strands of her short auburn hair. The hazel eyes looking back questioned her sanity. It was now or never. Part of her was encouraged by never.

How she got from the car to the steps of the porch, she didn't know. Kurt Simpson joined his daughter. There was no mistaking he was the father of the little girl. Her light brown hair and green eyes were the image of the tall man standing beside her. Chloe wondered what her mother had looked like.

Both Kurt and his daughter started down the stairs and Kurt reached out his hand to Chloe. "Hi, you must be Chloe."

"Of course she is, Dad," Meghan responded, rolling her eyes. "Hi, I'm Meghan."

Chloe couldn't help but smile as she shook Kurt's hand, and then reached for Meghan's outstretched one. The little girl didn't let go, so Chloe let them lead her back into the house.

"Meghan, take it easy," Kurt instructed. "We don't want to scare her away by showing your true, pushy self just yet."

Meghan rolled her eyes again. "Oh, Dad."

Meghan led Chloe to an overstuffed chair in a very cozy den and gave her a glass of lemonade. Then she left the room with a glass for herself.

Kurt took the third glass and sat across from Chloe. "Well, I guess it goes without saying,

that was my daughter, Meghan. She'll join us later. I won't be offended if you don't like the lemonade. Meghan made it and even if I supervised, I'm not exactly sure what's in it."

Chloe laughed. "Sounds like my nieces and nephews when they make their brews."

"Ah, so other children do the same experiments?" Kurt asked.

Chloe began to relax a little and her mouth wasn't quite so dry after trying the not so bad lemonade. "Yes, I've been the guinea pig for many experiments. I believe the last one was a drink made of orange soda, milk and mayo."

At the look on Kurt's face, she laughed. "Trust me, it tasted as bad as it sounds."

After an awkward moment, Chloe said, "You have a very nice home, Mr. Simpson."

"Please, call me Kurt, and thank you. My wife did most of the decorating."

Chloe caught a flicker of emotion pass on Kurt's face and then it was gone. He smiled as he pointed out the corner where the area was definitely for a child. "And Meghan designed that corner. I'm waiting for her to get older so she'll grow out of all that stuff and I can get rid of it."

Chloe wanted to respond, 'typical male', but decided against it. "Well, girls are into dolls, books and stuffed animals. Some stuff she'll grow out of, but others will stay with her forever." She was thinking of her own collection of stuffed animals that she never grew out of and how Andrew had always tried to get her to throw them away. Andrew. She pushed aside his image.

"Well, sir, the rest of your room is very comfortable with the furniture and HD TV. I can see why she has all her stuff in the corner of this room."

Kurt cleared his throat, "Okay, I guess we should get down to business."

"Ah, yes, good idea." Chloe held her breath and tried to be as open as possible.

He reached over and pulled a clipboard off the end table. The amiable conversation turned to business mode once he glanced at the papers in his hand.

"Let's see. The agency said that you have a very flexible schedule, which is just what I need. My wife died two years ago and my parents have been helping out a lot, along with other family members and friends. Now that my parents are moving to Florida and Meghan is older, I feel it's time to make some changes."

Chloe watched his hands as he spoke because she needed a break from his intense green eyes since they were a lot darker inside the house, almost a deep moss color. They were quite a contrast to his sandy hair.

"It's obvious that my daughter likes you because she isn't hovering, giving me the eye, or should I say rolling her eyes."

Chloe smiled. "You mean she trusts your judgment."

Kurt laughed. "Well at least she tries to give that impression. She's a bit overprotective of me. Sometimes I have to remind her who the adult is in the family."

Chloe found herself smiling again and relaxing more. *Hope.* Was it too soon to hope that this situation might work out after all?

He looked out the window and appeared to be seeing something Chloe couldn't. After a few seconds, he looked back at the clipboard. "Now, what experience do you have with children? I know you don't have any of your own, but you come highly recommended."

You don't have any children of your own.

Chloe pushed the crushing heartache as deep as she could and hoped it didn't show on her face. "Well, I have a few nieces and nephews that range in age from infant to sixteen years old. I've changed all of their diapers and have had them spend weekends with me to give their parents a break. We also take family vacations together."

Kurt smiled. "Well, I'd say that's a lot of experience. What I'm looking for is someone to be here when Meghan gets home from school, which will be around 3:15. I will be home between 5:00 and 7:00. Some days I'll take off and won't need you. I also work an occasional Saturday, but relatives or friends like to help out, unless of course you'd be interested."

He looked down at the paper again. Chloe was feeling hopeful as well as anxious. He spoke as if she had the job. But she knew that the true test would be spending time alone with Meghan, a stranger's child. After all, that's what adoption was about, taking a strange child into your care for life.

Kurt ran a hand through his hair, leaving a strand or two out of place. He smiled shyly as he looked back at her, causing her to fidget in her seat. He looked at the clipboard again and then put it back on the end table. "So, do you have any questions for me?"

Chloe wasn't prepared to ask questions, although she felt a strange desire to share all she'd been through with him and to explain why she was truly sitting in his den. Would he like the idea that his daughter was a guinea pig for her? She shuddered slightly at the thought. After all, it wasn't like she was diabolical or planning to cause any harm. It would be a test of her parenting ability. Besides, everyone she knew who had children said that there were no true reality handbooks on the subject, regardless of all the books out on the topic. Oh, how she wished there were some.

Since Kurt just sat there expectantly, she finally cleared her cluttered thoughts and asked, "What kind of routine does she have after school?"

Leaning back in his chair, he crossed a foot over his knee and clasped his hands on his stomach.

"Homework first, then possibly a snack, but only if she wants one. Limited television. She does have an X-box that I allow her to play once in awhile." He laughed at Chloe's expression. "Yes, she's very good at it. She's beaten me at several games. She's also too aggressive with it at times. If the weather is nice, I'd like her to be outside."

Chloe nodded and bit her lower lip. Her natural care taking instinct was kicking in, fighting for space with her feelings of inadequacy. A good sign she supposed. She reached for the lemonade to compose herself, took a sip and started choking.

Kurt was on his feet in an instant and was at her side even quicker.

"No, I'm okay," she sputtered, holding her hand out to ward him off. "It just went down the wrong way," she managed to say between coughs.

"Arms up," he commanded.

Her arms went up as she laughed and choked at the familiar command given to children choking.

Meghan appeared in the doorway. "Is everything okay?"

Chloe dropped her arms and the coughing began to subside. "Yes, I'm fine."

Kurt's eyes were warm with concern as he looked down at her. He finally went back to his chair and motioned for Meghan to join him. She sat on his lap and leaned her head on his shoulder.

Chloe's heart broke at the sight. Again, she pushed the familiar pain deep down.

Just as she was feeling exhaustion begin to overcome her, Kurt spoke.

"Are you sure you're okay?"

"Yeah," Meghan said. "You look sad."

Chloe blinked, putting on what she hoped was a happier look. "I'm fine. I love lemonade and drank it down too fast."

Meghan sat up. "Dad let me make it. Sometimes it's too tart."

Kurt pinched Meghan's cheek. "Just like you, eh?"

Meghan giggled and Chloe knew she had to get some air.

"So," Kurt said, "Do you think you'd be interested in the position?"

Hope and an overwhelming feeling of despair warred with Chloe, but Meghan was nodding her head up and down and pleading with the same green eyes as her Dad. Two sets of eyes like that didn't give a girl a chance. Not even a girl who was still wondering what the heck she was doing.

"I understand this is just until summer?" she asked.

Kurt nodded. "Once school is out I have other plans. With my parents moving to Florida sooner than expected, I just need help until then."

Chloe bit her lower lip again. "Well, if you think I'm the right person, then I will accept." Her thudding heart still made her question what she was doing.

Meghan got off her father's lap and walked over to Chloe, once again taking her hand and pulling her out of the chair.

"Come on. I'll show you my room."

"Meghan…"

"Its okay, Dad, I just want her to see it before she goes."

"It's all right, Mr. Simpson."

"Kurt."

She flushed. "Kurt. I can spare a couple of minutes before I leave."

Meghan led her out of the room, leaving Kurt alone.

Kurt shook his head as he watched his daughter lead her victim away. Leaning back in the chair and closing his eyes, a silent prayer was sent up to his wife and God. He never knew if he was doing the right thing with Meghan. She was growing so quickly. Not having his wife there was still deeply heart breaking.

Wiping his teary eyes, at least Chloe seemed to be able to help him in the short term before he took time off during the summer to be with his daughter. Then he would decide what to do with her once school started again.

His parents had always been there for him. He couldn't even think what it would be like without them around. Sherry at work was very willing to help, but he knew she wanted something from him that included more than time spent with his daughter. He couldn't give it to her because she was like a sister to him. She was part of a family that had taken care of him in his darkest days after his wife passed away.

Giggles brought him out of his thoughts and he dried his eyes again. He got up and headed to his daughter's room, certain that Chloe needed to be rescued.

Chloe had been telling Meghan a funny story about one of her nieces. They were still laughing when Kurt appeared in the doorway.

"Okay, you two. What's with all the laughing going on in here?"

Meghan frowned. "You said there should be more laughing, Dad, remember?"

Kurt turned a slight shade of pink and Chloe jumped in to diffuse the situation.

"I find that most people don't laugh enough, so your Dad is right." She winked at Meghan.

Meghan giggled. "I think he's just jealous that he missed out on what we were laughing at."

Kurt's eyes sent Chloe a warm thank you and then he narrowed them when looking at Meghan. "So, laughing without me, eh?" He grabbed Meghan and started tickling her. Laughter mingled with squeals of protest was contagious, so Chloe joined the laughter as well.

"Stop Daddy, okay, I give up."

The laughter died in Chloe but she kept a smile forced on her face, watching father and child calm down. *Stop Daddy.*

She cleared her throat. "Well, I can see that everything is under control. I'd better be on my way."

"You're taking the job, right?" Meghan asked.

"If your father still says its okay."

"He does."

"Meghan…"

"Sorry."

Kurt ruffled Meghan's hair. "Go have some X-box time while I walk Chloe to her car."

"Okay. Bye, Chloe. See you Monday."

"See you then," Chloe replied.

As they walked out of the house, Chloe said, "So I guess I start Monday?"

Kurt laughed. "Yes, if after all this, you're still interested."

Chloe smiled. "Yes, I am."

Kurt reached out his hand to shake Chloe's and she hesitated just a second before shaking it. He also handed her a key to the house.

"It's been nice meeting you, Chloe. I'll see you on Monday."

"Yes, boss."

It was Kurt's turn to roll his eyes. "Please, call me Kurt."

Chloe actually giggled. "Right. See you on Monday… Kurt."

She was back in her car, waving to him while driving away.

Kurt watched her go, wondering why the woman brought out such a protective urge in him. He certainly recognized the haunted eyes that appeared once again just before she left. He saw the same ones at times whenever he looked in the mirror.

*****

Chloe drove away in a head of fog. Tears swelled in her eyes as emotions meshed together with tears of joy and frustration. She survived the first step, but it drained her more than she thought it would.

Unfortunately, Andrew's face came to mind at that moment and deep resentment with it. Every time she tried to come to grips with what he did, anger got the best of her. Even after all the time that had passed, she still couldn't forgive him for abandoning her when she needed him most. She blamed him for forcing her into this unknown adventure.

In some ways she blamed God for the Andrew situation too and couldn't understand why all these things happened to her when she was a devoted believer.

It was nearly time for her psychological and physical therapy appointments. She was almost done with the physical, but knew the emotional piece would take a lot longer. Instead of driving home first, she went straight to her therapist,

Dr. Lambert. She needed to share her interview with the doctor who had helped her come such a long way. The therapist was part of a Catholic organization. The physical therapy for her leg and hand would be later in the day.

Once in the familiar, comfy chair she was used to, Chloe relaxed. Dr. Lambert walked in a few moments later. A petite woman in her forties, Dr. Lambert looked like a blonde Barbie doll. She was very fresh and energetic.

Dr. Lambert sat in the chair across from Chloe. "So, how did the interview go?"

Chloe slouched a bit in the chair. "Oh, my god, I can't believe I'm doing this."

Dr. Lambert smiled. "But you are doing it?"

"Yes."

"Good."

"Easy for you to say. I'm still not sure this is the right thing to do." She sat up straighter in the chair and began twisting her hands on her lap.

Dr. Lambert tilted her head.

"Oh, okay, it is the right thing to do. But she's not mine and no matter how it goes, she never will be and it just won't be the same."

"Tell me about the interview."

Chloe filled her in and once she was honest about the heartbreaking parts, the tears really came.

Dr. Lambert offered Chloe the tissue box and waited patiently for her to come to grips again.

"The thing is, I really like both of them," Chloe finally continued. "But I feel awkward not telling them why I'm truly doing this. Sometimes it felt like Mr. Simpson could see right through me."

"How is his daughter?

Chloe smiled. "Just like my niece, Candace, all sweetness on the outside and a little devil on the inside."

"And, Mr. Simpson?"

Chloe had to think for a moment as those warm green eyes came into view. "He's pleasant. Loves his daughter and, if I could read his face, misses his wife very much."

"Well, it sounds like you're off to a good start. Remember to take things one day at a time, Chloe. You've been through a lot and as good as this is for you, you still need to take care of yourself. How's the physical therapy going?"

"Good. I'm almost done. I think I have three more sessions."

"How does the leg feel?"

"Much better. Of course, the weather aggravates it at times. But I've lost the limp. My hand is pretty much back to normal," she explained, flexing both to prove her point.

Silence descended upon the two women. Even though Chloe was seeing Dr. Lambert less now, the main issue that Chloe always left for last, if at all, was Andrew. Chloe blew air out of her mouth. "Okay. I left the Simpson's very angry at Andrew for putting me in this predicament."

Dr. Lambert didn't respond.

"Okay, okay. I still resent him."

A slight smile appeared on Dr. Lambert's face.

"I don't want to talk about him."

Dr. Lambert shifted in her chair. "Well, I'd say this is the most you've said about him in awhile."

Chloe shrugged. "He's out of my life now. I'm trying to live mine without him, but…"

Dr. Lambert waited.

And waited.

"Jeez. I still don't know how to live without him, when he's still around and I'm where I am today because of him."

"Chloe, you're not giving yourself enough credit. Yes, you still have to learn to live with some of these things, but it's up to you where you go from here. He can only stop you if you let him."

Chloe's eyes began to fill again.

"It still hurts so badly. Sometimes it hurts more than the physical injuries." As she said the words, it wasn't Andrew's face that appeared before her, but Kurt Simpson's. *God help me.* Thoughts of his face full of concern when she choked on the lemonade suddenly appeared in the middle of her frustration.

Dr. Lambert cocked her head, as if noticing a change in Chloe, but she didn't say anything.

"Oh, I don't know. I'm just so impatient to get past all this painful stuff. Why does it take so long?"

Dr. Lambert smiled. "I'd say you're making great progress. Everyone has a different path to take when it comes to healing. You've had a double dose of physical and emotional healing to deal with. Again, I will say you're not giving yourself enough credit."

Taking deep breaths, Chloe nodded. "I am trying. I'm still grateful that I'm alive, but I don't understand why God has me on this path."

Dr. Lambert smiled. "Have you made it back to church yet?"

"No. I still can't bring myself to go. It's as if once I do...if I ever do...I'll accept what happened to me. As glad as I am to be alive, I still can't accept not being able to have a child."

"Well, Chloe, as time goes on, answers will come to you. One step at a time."

Chloe half laughed. "Right... one step at a time when I'd rather be running multiple steps to get to the answers a lot quicker."

Dr. Lambert smiled.

Chloe dabbed at her eyes once more, then stood to leave. "Well, now I get to go torture my body. Thanks for your time."

"You're very welcome. I think we'll make your next appointment in two weeks if that's okay with you."

"Really? Are you sure?"

Dr. Lambert got out of her chair and walked to the desk to get her appointment book. "Yes. But you can call anytime before then if you need me."

It truly didn't feel as bad as she thought it might. Spreading out her appointments had gone from twice a week to once a week and now longer. She trusted Dr. Lambert and would do what she suggested. Maybe it *was* time to give herself more credit for her recovery.

The two women shook hands and Chloe left. Now it was on to the torture chamber, although even that was beginning to be less annoying. Time did heal all wounds. It's just too bad it couldn't be done like the flick of a switch.

Too much emotion assailed her so far today. She stopped and got a small hot fudge sundae after the physical therapy session. It was a treat she indulged in when emotional and physical appointments were held on the same day. Adding the job interview increased the treat desire.

She arrived home ready to eat the sundae and maybe take a nap. Since it was Thursday, she had a few days to prepare herself for Monday. She flicked on the answering machine and sat on the sofa to eat.

The third message stopped the cherry covered spoonful on its way into her mouth.

Kurt Simpson was asking her to watch Meghan on Saturday. The spoon still hung in mid-air and then was put back into the ice cream. He apologized for the last minute request and wouldn't blame her if she couldn't do it.

Standing up and pacing while talking herself into doing this assignment earlier than Monday was a challenge. Finally, with shaking hands, she dialed his number and told him she'd be there. His scheduled sitter had to cancel.

After hanging up the phone, she paced a little more, talked to herself a lot more and then sat down to finish her sundae, which, for some reason, tasted better.

A hint of excitement tried to work its way into her, but caution kept it in perspective. After what Andrew had done, it was going to be hard to trust anything again.

Chapter 2

Saturday morning arrived quickly and Chloe was on her way to Kurt's for ten o'clock. He would need her until two. Meghan had a ballet class from eleven to twelve and even though Kurt could arrange to have Meghan go with a friend, Chloe volunteered to bring her.

Meghan was sitting on the porch, dressed in pink tights and a white sweatshirt. She looked like a sweet confection with sneakers on. Kurt was putting something in his car.

"Good morning," he called as she got out of the car.

"Good morning to you both. Don't you look pretty, Meghan".

Kurt finished putting stuff in his car and walked back to the porch. "I told her it was too early to get dressed, but she insisted on being ready by the time you arrived." He ruffled Meghan's hair as he went up the stairs and into the house.

Meghan and Chloe followed him.

"I've left directions to her class and money if you decide to go out for lunch. There's food here if you don't." Kurt hugged Meghan and grabbed the rest of his stuff. "I really appreciate this, Chloe. I'll be back by two or earlier."

Walking toward the door, he spoke to Meghan. "You behave yourself."

"I will."

"The number for the office is on the message board," he said as he went out the door.

"Okay." Chloe watched him drive away and fought a slight tingle of apprehension. When she turned from the door, Meghan was not around. She found her in the den, playing the X-box.

"There you are."

"Shh," Meghan replied. "I have to concentrate."

Chloe was fascinated as she watched the girl play the game. Kurt was right, she was very aggressive. After several minutes, she remembered that they had to leave for class soon.

"A few more minutes, Meghan, and then we have to go."

"Oh, no," Meghan exclaimed.

"What happened?"

Meghan looked at Chloe. "You made me lose my concentration."

Chloe was taken aback. "Um, sorry, I didn't mean to. I just don't want you to be late for your ballet class."

Meghan turned back to the game, pushing buttons and grumbling. "I don't feel like going now. I want to keep playing."

Before Chloe could answer, the doorbell rang and a voice called out, "Anybody home?"

"Sherry!" Meghan cried and abandoned the game to run and greet the woman.

Sherry caught Meghan in a hug as Chloe came up behind her. "Well, look at you, all ready to go dancing."

Meghan was back to her nice self. "Yeah, Chloe is taking me."

Chloe was watching the pretty young woman with the perfect body and long blond hair, wondering if she was friend or family.

Sherry reached out her hand. "Hi, I'm Sherry Ryan. I work for Meghan's father."

As they shook hands, Chloe said, "I'm Chloe Wheeler, and I guess I work for him too."

The two women laughed and then Chloe looked at Meghan.

"Okay, Meghan, do you have everything for class?"

"I'll get my bag."

Both women watched her go. Chloe called after her. "Don't forget to shut the X-box off."

Sherry's mouth dropped open and then she laughed.

"What?" Chloe asked.

"Is this your first time alone with her?"

"Yes, why?"

Sherry smirked. "Watch."

Meghan appeared with her bag and her eyes downcast. She looked up at Sherry first. "Sorry."

"I don't think I'm the one you should apologize to." She nodded at Chloe who looked puzzled.

"Sorry, Chloe."

Chloe looked askance at Sherry.

"X-box rules. No playing before noon on Saturday. Right, Meghan?"

"Yeah," she replied sheepishly.

Chloe wondered about Sherry knowing the rules, but then again, she did work for Kurt, so she probably helped out once in awhile. Her main concern now was that she had to make a decision on how to handle what Meghan had done. "Well, I guess you won't be playing it again today. We'll see what your father says beyond that."

Meghan's mouth dropped open and her eyes widened. "You're going to tell my Dad?"

"I think there's a good possibility."

"Oh."

"But we'll see how the rest of the day goes. Let's get you to class before we're late."

As the three of them walked out the door, Chloe paused. "I'm sorry, Sherry, was there something you wanted?"

"No, I stop by once in awhile to see if Kurt needs any help. I can see everything is under control."

Chloe wasn't sure, but there seemed to be an edge to the last sentence. Meghan was already at Chloe's car. "Can you come with us, Sherry?"

Sherry hesitated but Chloe said, "You're welcome to come if you want." Then she lowered her voice, "I think she's leery about being alone with me right now."

Sherry chuckled. "I think you're right." She yelled to Meghan, "I'll meet you there, sweetie, I can only stay a few minutes."

"All right." Hanging her head, she scraped her sneaker on the driveway.

The two women smirked as they made their way to their vehicles.

Sherry drove off first, yelling out the window, "See you there."

Chloe waved but Meghan just got in the car without a word. Small talk didn't get anywhere. Chloe was grateful that they only had a 5 minute ride.

Sherry was getting out of her car as Chloe and Meghan arrived. All three walked into the dance studio and then Meghan left to join her classmates. Chloe and Sherry found seats. Though there seemed to be a curious air between the two women, neither got to say much because the class began.

Halfway through the class, Kurt showed up. The class took a five minute break and Meghan lit up when she saw her father, and then she became subdued once again. Chloe also noticed that Meghan wasn't the only one who lit up when Kurt arrived. *So there is something between him and Sherry?* An increase in her own pulse made her wonder what her problem was.

Meghan gave Chloe a half glance as she hugged her father. After a few moments it was time go back to class. Kurt got in a quick hello to the ladies as he sat and watched the rest of the class.

When class was over, Meghan went straight to her father. "Are you done working, Dad?"

"No, I just wanted to see you. I'm heading back, but I'll be done before two."

Sherry closed the distance between herself and Kurt. "Is there anything I can do to help?"

Kurt looked at Chloe and then back at Sherry. "No, I just need to finish up a couple of things."

"Are you sure?"

"Yes, I'm sure."

They all started to walk out together. Chloe's mind was racing at that peculiar exchange. As they walked into the bright sunlight, Meghan said to Sherry, "I thought you couldn't stay for the whole class?"

Sherry flushed a little. "I decided you were more fun to watch."

An odd silence hung in the air.

"Dad?"

"Yes, Meghan."

"Can I talk to you before you go back to work?"

"I'll meet you at the car," Chloe said.

"And I'll see you all later," Sherry said as she walked to her car.

Several minutes later, Kurt and Meghan walked toward Chloe. They made a cute picture walking hand and hand. The only thing missing was Sherry walking with them. Or for that matter, any woman, making the picture complete. She tamped down the tug at her heart.

Meghan had a smile on her face as she approached Chloe, but it was Kurt who spoke. "We were just discussing if you would like to join us for dinner tonight."

"Oh, um. I don't know."

"Do you have other plans?" Megan asked.

"Ah, no."

"Then can you join us, please?"

Chloe was caught off guard and Kurt seemed to take on a different color. "Sorry, I know it is last minute. Maybe we can do it another time and of course, your husband or significant other could join us as well."

Meghan glared at her father.

Chloe actually smiled. "No, there's no husband or anyone and yes, I'd love to join you tonight." What was she thinking?

Kurt relaxed and Meghan smiled. "Okay then, I'll see you two in a little while."

"Bye, Dad."

"See you later", was all Chloe could say.

On the drive home, Meghan was more like the child Chloe first met. "So, where do you want to go for lunch?"

"Let's go home since we're going out tonight."

"Okay, sounds good to me."

They went back to the house and had peanut butter and jelly sandwiches along with potato chips and milk. It was a meal from Chloe's childhood that made her feel warm and cozy. The unexpected comfort feeling was magnified when she and Meghan went outside to the swings.

There were two large, homemade wooden swings hanging from sturdy oak branches. They each took one and had a contest to see how high they could go. It was wonderful. Chloe felt like a child again. She leaned back like she did as a child and just let the wind take her. Laughter escaped from her and when she closed her eyes, was transported back in time. Meghan's laughter became her best friend Patti's laughter.

They were wonderful, freeing memories. She sat up straight when Meghan called for her to pay attention and the two of them continued to swing higher.

A few minutes later they slowed down while dragging their feet on the grass and twisting the swings back and forth.

After a minute, Meghan spoke. "Chloe, is your Mom still living?"

"Yes."

Meghan frowned a bit. "You're lucky. I miss mine even though I can't always remember her anymore." She shrugged a little. "I know God is taking care of her, but I still don't understand why He took her away."

Chloe's heart sank and she had to fight back some unexpected tears. "I'm very sorry for your loss, Meghan." She couldn't look directly into the child's eyes but knew the comfort priority was for the child, not herself.

Meghan continued to twist in the swing while kicking the grass. "Dad explained things to me, but I still don't get it."

Chloe still struggled to focus only on the child.

Meghan stopped her swing and looked directly at Chloe. "Will you be mad at God when he takes your Mom?"

Chloe was not prepared for that question. Tears were getting out of control and all she could do was nod yes.

Meghan started to swing some more. "Guess he calls people when he wants to. I wish he'd asked me first."

This brought a reluctant smile to Chloe as she began to swing as well. Re-focusing on her own situation, she couldn't help agreeing with that question. At least it was an opportunity to have a child born taken away, not a child itself. Part of her struggle seemed to lessen a small bit. She still had her life even though it was sent in an unthinkable direction.

The conversation ended and the swinging contest began again.

That's how Kurt found them when he arrived home. Memories of Meghan and his wife, as well as himself at times, assailed him as he watched them behaving so carefree. A dull ache tugged at his heart, but there was something a little different with the pain this time. He wasn't sure why, but he could still breathe when he felt it. Maybe he was on the threshold of a different level of healing.

After taking a deep breath, he headed out the door toward the girls. Both were still laughing as he approached.

Chloe's heart skipped a beat as she watched Kurt walk toward them.

"Hi Dad, come push us."

Kurt laughed. "You seem to be doing fine by yourselves."

Meghan slowed down. "Yeah, but it's more fun if you push."

He ruffled her hair as he took his place behind her. "You're just being lazy," he said, as he sent her into the air.

Meghan giggled. "Slow down, Chloe, so my Dad can push you."

Chloe slowed down as her heart beat faster, especially when Kurt grabbed her around the waist instead of the ropes. "Ready?"

"Ready."

He pulled her back and let her fly. Then he stood between the two and pushed them on their backs.

Chloe was having fun in a simple sort of way. She was feeling lighter and happier than she had in awhile. As much as other thoughts tried to intrude, she kept them at bay. The good moments needed to be cherished as they happened.

"Higher, Dad. Use both hands."

"And deprive Chloe?"

"She can do it herself now."

"Gee, thanks," Chloe responded with a laugh as she pumped her legs. After a few minutes of flying through the air and listening to father and daughter laugh, she knew it was time to go. Reluctantly she slowed to a stop.

"Why are you stopping, Chloe?" Meghan asked.

"It's time for me to go." She stood and faced the still swinging child and her father. "Where am I meeting you tonight?"

Before Kurt could answer, Meghan said, "Dad, it's your turn on the swing." Kurt stopped pushing Meghan long enough to sit on the vacated swing. "How about if we go to China Garden around six-thirty?"

"Yeah," Meghan yelled.

"Sure," Chloe responded. "Good choice. It's the best Chinese food restaurant in Connecticut."

"Chloe, can you give me and Dad a push before you go?"

Chloe stepped behind Meghan and grabbed the ropes.

"No, you have to grab my waist so it's like pushing *me*, not the swing."

Chloe grabbed the girl's waist, pulled her back as high as she could and let go.

"Good one, Chloe, now Dad."

Chloe hesitated a moment, but figured Meghan would make her do it correctly if she reached for the ropes. Feeling heat rise in her face, she reached for Kurt and sent him into the air as well.

From behind them, she said, "Have fun you two, I'll see you tonight." She walked away without looking at them, still feeling the warmth in her face.

"Bye," they said together.

Chloe left hearing Meghan giving her father instructions on how to pump his legs properly. Once in her car, she sat for a moment and took a deep breath. How could she feel so comfortable in that scene? It was make believe. The reality was that she still wasn't getting married or having a child of her own. There was no doubt she could care for Meghan, but the child wasn't hers. Doubts assailed her regarding the adoption plans. Adoption was so final. What if, in the end, she couldn't deal with raising the child of another person, regardless of how much love she could share? Maybe it would be better if she didn't go to dinner tonight, no matter how strongly she wanted to. Why was she doing this to herself?

She drove away feeling very agitated. On the other hand, she needed to re-focus. Once she arrived home, she went to work on her computer. Since the accident, the computer company she had worked for set her up at home so she could still work and recover at the same time. Developing computer programs was her gift and the company didn't want to lose her. It still gave her something to do especially since she didn't need any money, thanks to the settlement from the accident. She had no specific hours anymore, but did the assignments as quickly as she could in between things.

Two hours engrossed in work did her a world of good. It put some things in perspective. She was actually now looking forward to dinner with Kurt and Meghan. It was always easy for her to hide from things she was afraid of. There was nothing threatening in having dinner with them. Of course, if she thought about it long enough, she would find something.

After a little more time at the computer, she took a shower and got ready for dinner.

She was very glad it was springtime now and summer around the corner.

Chloe arrived at the restaurant on time, criticizing herself for the rollercoaster emotions of the day. *All goes with the recovery territory.* She was going to have a nice dinner, go home and relax for the rest of the weekend, and then start on her new job on Monday. Detachment is what she would practice.

Kurt waved to her as she walked into the restaurant. Approaching the table she noticed another person. Sherry. What was she doing here? So much for detachment, she thought as her heart sank a bit.

"Hi, Chloe," Meghan said as she pushed into the booth making room for Chloe. Chloe noticed that Sherry was very close to Kurt, her long blonde hair brushing his arm.

"Hi everyone."

"We get to use chopsticks tonight. Dad thinks I'm ready to try them again."

They placed their orders and Kurt started showing Meghan how to use them. She had tried in the past, but wasn't very good.

"So, Chloe," Sherry said. "How long have you been taking care of children for a living?"

Kurt and Meghan dropped the chopsticks and looked at Sherry.

Sherry shrugged and raised her eyebrows. "What? Did I say something wrong?"

Kurt leveled a look at her as Chloe sat stunned at the challenge in the question. This was not the same Sherry she met earlier that day. He said, "Let's not discuss work. We're here to have dinner."

Sherry shrugged with a laugh. "Sorry, I didn't mean anything by it."

Chloe knew differently and if her guess was right, so did Kurt. What was going on between the two of them?

The food arrived and Chloe picked up the chopsticks, using them flawlessly.

Meghan watched her with awe. "Wow, Chloe, you can use those really good. Can you help me?"

Chloe looked at Kurt. "Sure. Your Dad gave you a good lesson. You just need to practice."

Meghan tried to pick up a piece of chicken and the sticks crossed, sending the chicken into Chloe's plate. Everyone laughed. Both Kurt and Chloe reached over to show her how to do it and their hands collided. Everyone laughed again, except for Sherry. On the second try, Meghan was able to get the chicken into her mouth successfully.

The rest of the meal went well, and when they finished having dessert, everyone got a fortune cookie and then it was time to leave.

"Well, thanks for inviting me," Chloe said, as they walked out of the restaurant. She turned to Sherry. "It was nice to see you again."

Sherry was standing close to Kurt. "Same here." Somehow Chloe doubted it.

"See you Monday, Chloe," Meghan said as she waved.

"See you Monday."

When Chloe got home, she worked on the computer again before heading to bed. Determined to make things work with her new job, she resolved herself to the fact that Sherry was interested in Kurt and for some reason was threatened by her being around him. Why Kurt didn't return the interest, she didn't know. Well, that was their problem; she had enough of her own.

Across town, Kurt had put his daughter to bed and was sitting on the back porch thinking over the day.

"Please, Lord, help me to trust you again with my life."

He was warming up to the fact that Chloe would be good for his daughter. But there were questions regarding her affect on him. He couldn't deny a stirring within himself that hadn't been there for a long time. Unfortunately, Sherry must have noticed something as well, if her manner at dinner meant anything.

Leaning back in the chair, head against the house, he let out a long sigh. There was more to Chloe than met the eye. The desire to get to know her was strong. Maybe as he got to know her he could help remove the haunted look he could still see in her eyes. And maybe, he was out of his own mind.

Chapter 3

Screaming woke up Chloe. After several deep breaths, she realized she was the screamer. It was the accident nightmare. Only this time there were a few new parts to it that she tried not to focus on. Since she had started to remember more of that terrible day, she was surprised the dream hadn't happened sooner. Regardless, she was still shaken. It was four in the morning and now she is totally awake. It seemed to be a race between the baby dream and the accident nightmare to see which was going to drag her down less as time went on. Maybe once she remembered all of the accident, it would be purged from her dreams. Or maybe it would increase them. Who knows how these things really work. But the baby dream would probably never go away, since the fact she couldn't ever have one wouldn't change.

She got up and went to the computer, hoping it would keep her mind off bad thoughts. Researching adoption options as well as taking a look at a computer disk from her boss, made time fly by. She still felt a little guilty about not letting Kurt know she still worked for the company she was with at the time of the accident.

At six o'clock she was still at it. By seven she was in the shower. While in the shower, for some reason she decided to go to church. Why, she didn't know. She was still struggling with her relationship with God, even though she knew he was with her on a daily basis.

As she got closer to the church, her nerves kicked in enough to cause her to only drive by while Father Richmond was on the steps greeting parishioners.

As she turned around to go back home, her mouth dropped open and her heart skipped a beat as she saw Kurt and Meghan going into the church. Her mind went in different directions trying to recall if she remembered ever seeing them there. She did not, but was surprised at her strong desire to join them. Unfortunately, it still wasn't enough to change her mind.

Returning home, she listened to a couple of phone messages. Her heart nearly stopped when she heard Andrew's voice. He was her ex-fiancé, who abandoned her after such a devastating car accident. Laughing hysterically, she was very glad she hadn't walked into the church earlier. The joke would've been so much crueler. Hearing his voice almost sent all her therapy out the window. Almost. Sliding down the wall in the hallway and sitting on the floor, tears overtook her. After a good, cleansing cry, she got up and listened to the message again. She couldn't imagine why Andrew wanted to see her again. Deciding not to call him back, she returned the other call from her friend, Patti, and tried to focus on her new nanny job. Luckily no other unexpected events popped into the rest of her day.

Monday morning she awoke to a sunny day with no bad dreams that she could remember. After more adoption research and some computer job work, nerves kicked in again as she got ready to head to Kurt's.

Once at his place, Chloe was waiting for Meghan like an anxious parent. A classmate's mother gave

Meghan a ride home every day. Nothing was ever mentioned about the X-box issue, so Chloe hoped there wouldn't be another scene. To her relief, Meghan was very glad to see her and once settled, started in on her homework. And that's pretty much how the first week went. To her surprise, concerns about being with Meghan began to pale against the concerns she began having about Kurt.

He convinced her to stay for supper two nights, even though she needed to keep her distance emotionally. Meghan was her job, and being around Kurt shifted the important focus that Chloe needed to survive.

When Friday arrived and he asked her to go out to dinner with them, she turned him down. Both father and daughter were very disappointed, but she held her ground. She would see them on Monday.

Andrew tried to reach her a few more times but she refused to return his calls even though her gut was telling her to contact him and get it over with. Dread at what he would say kept her from calling. If she was honest with herself, she liked the time spent with Kurt and Meghan too much. A lot of laughing went on this past week and she didn't want to spoil it with bad memories.

After spending Saturday afternoon with her friend Patti, and the two of them tried to figure out what Andrew wanted, Chloe decided to bite the bullet and call him. She agreed to meet with him Sunday afternoon. To her dismay, it was nice to hear his voice again. As angry as she was at him, she had to admit that even the messages he had left still touched a place in her heart. Well, what had she been telling the therapist all along? It was hard to live life without him when he was still around. The pain was deep when she thought about him breaking off their engagement because she couldn't have children. It was an accident, for God's sake. But Andrew wanted children of his own, not someone else's when you didn't know what their genes were like. Even now, when she thought she had come to terms with it, it gnawed at her. She had truly loved him. Probably still did, but that didn't change a thing.

Chloe was up most of the night wondering what it was going to be like seeing him after so much time had passed. They had agreed to meet at a local restaurant.

Finally getting a few hours sleep before getting ready for the meeting, she chided herself once up and getting ready, about trying to look awesome.

She always looked good and didn't need to go out of her way for the man who abandoned her when needed the most.

Andrew was already there when Chloe arrived. Her heart skipped a beat and then thudded as she pushed the pain away.

He stood when Chloe approached the table. "Hi Chloe."

"Hello Andrew." Chloe avoided his outstretched hand and slid into the booth.

A waitress handed her a menu that she put aside and just ordered an ice water. Hunger was not an issue at the moment. They both stared at each other and then Andrew cleared his throat.

"I'm glad you agreed to meet with me."

"What do you want, Andrew?"

He shrugged. The laugh lines around his blue eyes seemed deeper than she remembered. His dark hair still beckoned her to touch it. It had been four months since she last saw him.

Chloe stared at him. "You already apologized the last time I saw you."

"Well, I want to apologize again." He looked straight at her. "I miss you."

No, no, no. Chloe sucked in a breath and almost forgot to let it out. "What are you talking about?"

"Come on, Chloe. Are you going to make this more difficult than it already is?"

"Me? Let's not compare notes on difficulties, Andrew. What do you want?"

Chloe fidgeted as he assessed her, and then blurted, "I want you back."

Shocked silence.

"What?"

"You heard me. Are you going to make me beg?"

Chloe stopped fidgeting, only because she was frozen. Was this guy for real? "Andrew, I don't understand."

He leaned forward, with hands folded on the table. "I still want to marry you."

Chloe opened her mouth and then closed it again. This had to be a joke, another cruel joke.

Andrew continued, "I know I've treated you badly. Believe me I've paid for it."

What was that supposed to mean, Chloe wondered? Even through her fog, she could sense this was about him and not her. "What about children?"

He shrugged again. "I can live without them."

Chloe blinked and then closed her eyes. Reaching as deep as she could, she said, "Well, I can't."

His blue eyes clouded over. Chloe braced herself for the storm that would come with that look. She didn't have long to wait.

"You've been taking care of another man's child, pretending she's yours."

Chloe's world tilted a bit, but she righted herself. "Excuse me?" She couldn't bring her thoughts together. *Come on, Chloe.*

"Are you going to deny it?" He asked, with a penetrating stare.

Chloe looked down at the menu that was never opened. After several long seconds, she looked straight back at him. "What concern is it of yours what I am doing with my life?"

"Don't evade the question, Chloe. You can't have your own child so you're using someone else's?"

Chloe blinked, still fighting the sinking feeling. "You think that's funny bringing that up to me? You're sick."

"And you still haven't answered the question."

"The answer is no. How absurd. I'm taking care of a child for a few hours a week. And again, why is it any of your business?" How did he know what she was up to?

Andrew sat back with a smirk on his face. "I have my ways. I've also heard that you aren't seeing anyone."

"So."

"So, it isn't normal for you to be alone after what you've been through. You need someone to take care of you, and I'm the one. I've always been the one, and you know it."

Chloe blinked again. "Why now, Andrew, after all this time? Why now, when you should have been with me through all of the surgeries and therapies I've had to go through? As bad as I've felt, this is not the answer I've wanted."

He shrugged. "I've realized how wrong I've been."

Chloe knew then and there that he was lying. Andrew never admitted to being wrong about anything. Something was going on and she didn't want to stay around to find out what it was. Standing up with a determination that surprised her, she said, "I'm leaving. You've caused enough pain in my life, Andrew, and I want you to stay away from me. I don't know what you're about, but I'm out of here."

She walked away, barely able to feel her legs, hoping she wouldn't embarrass herself in some way. As she got into the car, her name was called. She ignored it as she got inside, and then she looked up to see Meghan running toward her. Kurt was right behind her. She rolled the window down as Meghan arrived. "Hi Chloe, did you eat here too?"

"Yes, I'm finished and on my way."

Andrew had come out looking for her. As Kurt arrived behind Meghan, Chloe pleaded with her eyes for him to take the child away. He turned in time to see where Chloe was looking.

"Come on, Meghan, looks like Chloe already ate. We'll see her tomorrow."

"Yes you will."

As soon as the two were away from the car, Chloe drove off. From the corner of her eye through the side mirror, she saw Sherry walking up the steps of the restaurant. But instead of going in to join Meghan and Kurt, she stopped to talk to Andrew. Tingles ran through her body. No way, she thought. A strong premonition assailed her as well. If she gave in to what she was thinking, she'd think she was set up. *Keep driving.*

Instead of going home, she went to her best friend Patti's house. Patti answered the door. "What's wrong?"

Chloe chuckled. "Gee, can you tell?"

The two went and sat in the living room. "Do you want something to drink?" Patti asked as she continued to braid her long red hair.

"No thanks. I just thought I'd stop by and tell you about my disastrous meeting with Andrew."

"Oh no. I guess maybe I shouldn't have encouraged you to go."

"Right now, I'd say yes, but at the time..." she paused, looking over Patti's shoulder. "I don't know what I expected, but it wasn't what ended up happening."

Chloe filled her in, even on the absurd idea that Sherry had something to do with it.

"You said Sherry works for Kurt?"

"Yeah."

Patti shrugged. "Maybe she and Andrew just met each other recently."

"It's possible. I don't remember her being around when we were together, but that doesn't mean they didn't already know each other."

Chloe still felt uneasy about seeing the two of them together, although she was pretty sure the woman was there because of Kurt.

Chloe and Patti spent the rest of the visit catching up with each other's family and friend situations.

When Chloe headed home, she was still tortured about something going on between Sherry and Kurt, but was able to get more computer work done before going to bed with a grateful dreamless sleep.

The next day at Kurt's, her thoughts were confirmed. Meghan told her that Sherry's parents had invited them all to dinner. She relaxed a little, criticizing herself for being so paranoid.

Meghan didn't have any homework, so they decided to take a walk.

As they walked along, Megan asked, "What did you have for dinner last night?"

Before Chloe could answer, she asked another question, "Who did you eat with?"

She hated to lie. "I just had a chicken salad with a friend."

"A boyfriend?"

Hesitating and squashing that connotation took some effort. "No, just a friend."

"Oh. You know what I think?"

Oh, no, here it comes. "What?"

"I think Sherry likes my Dad."

No kidding, Chloe wanted to say. "Well, she does work for him."

Meghan was kicking stones off the sidewalk. "I know. But I think it's more than that."

Chloe stopped. "Why would you think that?" She knew children were perceptive, but at eight years old?

Meghan cocked her head and shrugged. "It's just a feeling."

They started walking again. "Oh. Does it bother you, Meghan, that your Dad is interested in someone?"

Meghan ran to the edge of the sidewalk to pick up a penny. Chloe hoped that would change the subject. Wishful thinking. "No, but I don't think he feels the same way."

Chloe tried to figure out how to change the subject as Meghan gave her the penny and said, "If you find a penny with the head up, you're supposed to give it to someone for good luck."

Chloe smiled. "Thank you. That's very nice of you." As they continued walking, no more was said about Kurt and Sherry. When they returned to the house, Kurt was home. "Meghan, Casey called to see if you want to go over for dinner."

"Can I Dad?"

"Sure, as long as your homework is done."

"Didn't have any today."

Kurt called Casey's Mom as Meghan headed out the door to the neighbors. Once she was gone, he looked at Chloe. "Would you like to join me for dinner?"

Chloe hesitated. "I don't think so. I've got to get back home."

Kurt nodded. "Okay." He fidgeted a little. "Ah... Chloe. I don't want to intrude where it's none of my business, but is everything okay? I mean, last night?"

Chloe suddenly wanted to pour her heart out to the man, but she held back. He really didn't need to know what she was up to and why. "I'm fine. I'm sure that looked a little strange, but everything is just fine." She turned to leave.

"Chloe?"

"Yes," she responded without turning.

"I'm here if you ever need to talk." She turned back around and smiled. "Thanks, I appreciate that." Then she left.

It took all her strength to keep walking and not turn and go back to him. Dangerous. Very dangerous. She didn't want to think about how he'd respond if he knew the truth. She also didn't want to think about what would happen if she bared her soul to him. The fact of seeing him and

Meghan going into the church was not brought up either.

Kurt watched her drive away. He wasn't hungry all of a sudden. He was alone. Very alone. He still couldn't help feeling that there was more to Chloe than met the eye. He almost wanted to shake her and make her talk to him. Of course, he had no right. But he was good with people, and something was up with the woman. He needed to release some energy. Turning away from the door, he headed to the den to play the X-box.

That's where Meghan found him when she returned home.

"Can I play, Dad?"

"Not this time."

"Why not?"

"Because I want to play by myself."

"But, Dad…"

"Meghan, please. Just leave me alone for a bit."

Meghan left the room in a huff. Kurt felt a little guilty, but she'd get over it. Everything wasn't always about her.

Kurt finished taking his frustrations out on the game and then, feeling guilty for sending his daughter away, went to find Meghan.

She was watching television in the living room with her 'I can't believe Dad blew me off look'.

"Meghan?"

"What."

"You can have a turn now."

"I don't want to play," she said, folding her arms and pouting.

Kurt sat next to her and she moved away. He tried to keep the smile to himself, as he followed her.

"Dad," she said as she pushed him.

"Come on, Meg, I'm sorry, all right? I just needed to work off some frustration."

Still not looking at him, she replied, "You're always working off frustration." She got up and left the room in another huff.

Kurt's smile left his face. Was he? He leaned back against the sofa and stared sightless at the television. His world was changing. Meghan was older. His parents were moving. Business was good. But something was missing. Something he didn't think he'd truly want in his life again, at least not until Meghan was grown up. Chloe. Chloe's simple presence had kindled a longing inside of him. A longing he thought never to feel again. But she was also a mystery. He chuckled. Most women were. However, his gut told him that the mystery wasn't the ordinary kind and the curious side of him was getting stronger as he got to know her better.

He sighed and stood up. Clicking off the television, he went to find his daughter once again.

Chloe would only be around for a few more weeks and then his summer plans kicked into gear. Whatever secrets the lady had, were more than likely none of his business anyway. In spite of that feeble attempt at reality, he was as determined to find out what made her tick as he was to heed the nagging warning to stay away.

God help him if he was falling for the girl.

Chapter 4

Chloe's heart and mind were so scrambled now about Andrew and Kurt, she was determined to push them both aside so she could focus on a potential child. Thinking of the adoption possibility was complicated enough without those guy situations coming at her unexpectedly. At first she felt the meeting with Andrew was such a bad thing because he was up to no good. Then she felt it just made her more committed to looking into adoption, *alone.* Knowing she could rely on family and friends to assist her with the child was encouraging for her. It was important that a child has several supporters.

Her psychologist had given her some church adoption group information to start with as well as mentioned that she may want to think about foster care as well.

She began searching online and even found some organizations in the phone book. She was surprised at how many there were along with the legalities and costs. Not that a child's life should come cheap or unprotected.

She also did some research into surrogate mothers, but didn't know if she could stand to watch someone go through the pregnancy stages when she would never go through them herself. Open adoptions had her nervous about the biological parents getting involved with the child and possibly wanting them back. Foster care was only temporary, even though it was a necessary thing for some kids, getting close to them and then letting them go would be too hard to contemplate.

The week was going by uneventfully for a change, and by the end of the week, Chloe wondered for the millionth time why she was doing this. It was just as permanent as birthing a child your self. She slouched on the sofa and rubbed her eyes, which watered from the strain of looking at the computer so long. After closing her eyes for a few moments, she opened them and looked around her spacious work and living area.

She had a nice home to offer a child. Financially secure, thanks to the settlement she received from the accident, the child would never want for anything.

Slouching further into the sofa, she wiped her eyes again and sighed. All the money in the world could not replace what was taken from her. But spending time with Meghan had shown her that anything was possible, and nothing was guaranteed. Siblings and friends advised her to start with love and deal with whatever comes on a daily basis. Her accident was a perfect example of having to deal with the unexpected.

Hope. As overwhelming as all the information was that she was gathering, she had hope deep in her soul.

The phone rang and she answered on the third ring. It was Kurt asking her to join him and Meghan at their favorite Chinese food place again.

Chloe hesitated, thinking of the last time they went there, but agreed. After all, what could it hurt and she had the day off because sometimes Kurt took Fridays off. The chances of Sherry being there again was just something she would have to deal with. She also felt entitled to at least enjoy that little something extra she was feeling deep down inside, safe and protected with no chance to explore.

They all arrived at the restaurant at the same time. There was no sign of Sherry, but that didn't mean anything.

Once they were seated and had ordered, Kurt looked at her.

"Are you looking for someone?"

Chloe flushed a little and didn't know what to say.

Meghan said it for her. "Sherry isn't coming, if that's what you think."

Chloe blinked and just marveled at the intuition of the child. All she could say was, "Oh".

Kurt smiled at her. "Sherry works for me, Chloe, and her family has been very good to me. But that's all there is to it."

"She likes you, Dad," Meghan blurted out.

Both Kurt and Chloe stared at her, causing her to shrug. "Well, she does."

Chloe felt her cheeks burning. What a conversation to be having.

"Hi Chloe," a familiar voice said.

Gratefully and reluctantly, Chloe looked up at her other boss and his wife.

"Hi Mr. Crane. How are you Cindy?"

Mr. Crane pulled a computer disk out of his coat pocket. "I hope you don't mind if I give you this here. I was going to drop it off at your house after we ate."

Chloe took the disk, well aware of the curiosity in the air generated by Meghan and Kurt. She made quick introductions. "Thanks, I'll work on it first thing in the morning."

"Okay, nice to meet you folks; enjoy your dinner."

"You, too," Chloe responded.

Mr. Crane and his wife had been stand in parents for her after the accident and knew what she was up to. Her own parents had gone back to California after staying with her when the accident first happened.

Their food arrived and even though Chloe dug in, both Kurt and Meghan were still looking at her.

She put her fork down. "Okay. I'm a computer programmer. I have been for seven years." She shrugged. "Don't worry; it won't interfere with my taking care of Meghan."

"So, how come you wanted to take care of me, if you already have a job?" Meghan asked as she put food in her mouth. She was very good with the chopsticks now.

Chloe glanced at Kurt, who she could tell was wondering the same thing. Believe it or not, now she was half hoping Sherry would show up. Or anybody for that matter.

"Well, the truth is, computers are machines and as much as I like the work, there isn't a lot of people contact. I happen to love children and just thought I should do something else worthwhile."

"Why was he going to drop it off at your house? Don't you work in an office?" Kurt asked.

"I do a lot of work at home, away from distractions. Sometimes I go into the office."

When she looked at him, her heart sank. He didn't believe her.

"Dad, you haven't eaten anything."

He didn't take his eyes off of her, but they were narrowed a bit now.

Finally breaking eye contact, he looked at his plate. Chloe saw the effort it took for him to start eating. What was she going to do now if he pursued his questioning? She looked at Meghan. "You're doing really well with the chopsticks."

"Thanks. I think I need to go to the bathroom."

"Sure, sweetie, I'll go with you."

As they walked away, Chloe felt Kurt's eyes on her and a shiver ran through her body.

Kurt watched the two go and forced himself to take a deep breath. Chloe was hiding something very important. Parental protection kicked in really strong. Should he question her? Her private life was her business, but if it affected his daughter in any negative way, he wouldn't forgive himself. Right now the only danger he could see was his daughter getting attached to the woman. He could understand that himself. Red warning flags were everywhere now and he didn't know how to deal with them. After all, what did it matter that she had another job? Some people had multiple jobs. But wouldn't it have come up at some point in a discussion? And hadn't he always wondered in the back of his mind why someone her age wanted to take care of a child part time?

He watched the two of them coming back to the table and his heart did a little flip. Maybe he was just imagining things.

"Hey Dad. Casey and her parents are here too. Can I go have dessert with them?"

Chloe's palms began to sweat. Having to be with Kurt one on one was not in her plans.

"Finish your dinner and then you can go over." He waved to them once Meghan pointed them out.

She finished her meal in record time and then left the table.

Chloe focused on her food, very aware of the curiosity between them. Kurt still wasn't touching his food.

"Not that it really matters what you do with your own time, Chloe, but why didn't you tell me about your other job?"

Chloe let out a breath and shrugged. "It's really not a big deal. It won't interfere with Meghan, I promise you."

"But, seven years? That's a long time to be with a company. I have friends that are programmers, and though some may take their work home with them, they spend the majority of time in an office or traveling."

Chloe laughed. "Well, getting to work at home is a perk for being with the company for so long. I'm also on good terms with my boss and his wife."

Kurt didn't say anything, but his furrowed brow told her he still wasn't satisfied.

She continued to eat the tasteless food and scrambled to come up with something else to talk about. Then she remembered she was spending Saturday with her sister, Sandy and her daughter, Candace. Candace's younger sister, Terry, was staying with a friend for the weekend. Gathering her wits, she jumped in with a suggestion.

"Since we've got a minute without Meghan, what would you say to me stealing her tomorrow?" Oh God, did she really use that word?

She smiled at the look on Kurt's face. "I mean borrow her." Jeez, she wasn't doing very well. She rolled her eyes and continued. "I'm spending the day with my sister and her nine year old daughter. We're going to Slater Park in Rhode Island and a movie. Not necessarily in that order, but I thought Meghan might enjoy it."

Kurt visibly relaxed and said, "I'll have to ask her. I try to let her make her own decisions about things like that. Sometimes she jumps to the occasion but then changes her mind. I think she feels guilty about leaving me alone."

That nearly brought tears to Chloe's eyes. It must be difficult for Meghan not having her mother around. Even though she's a child, and a stubborn one at times, she was still fragile and wanted to take care of her father.

Whatever tension had been between the two had eased a bit but still hovered.

Meghan and the neighbors came by the table and Meghan slid into the booth next to Chloe.

They exchanged greetings and introductions and then everybody left the restaurant.

In the parking lot Kurt asked Meghan if she wanted to spend Saturday with Chloe. At first she said yes and then her face clouded over as the now familiar struggle of leaving her father was noticeable to Chloe.

"Maybe your father can join us at some point if you want."

Meghan seemed to think on it and then said, "Do you want to Dad?"

Kurt knelt down to be eye to eye with his daughter. "I've actually got some work to finish up, so why don't you just go and have a good time?"

Chloe's heart tumbled as she watched the scene between father and daughter. Why did it always hit her at the strangest times? She was stronger than this, but it was such a moving scene that she just wanted to hug them both and tell them it would be okay.

God, these moments are beyond heart breaking. I appreciate still being alive but still struggle with not being able to have my own child.

Kurt took his finger and traced a smile on Meghan's face.

"Okay, Dad, if you're sure."

He stood up. "Yes, I'm very sure, honey."

They both looked at Chloe and Kurt said, "Why don't I drop her off at your place after her dance lesson?"

Chloe snapped out of her fog. "Ah, well, I can pick her up at your place."

There was that look on Kurt's face again. "Well, you've done enough for us. It's the least I can do."

"Yeah Chloe. I want to see where you live," Meghan said, excitedly.

Chloe didn't know why she didn't want them to go to her house, her personal space, but she couldn't come up with a good enough reason. "Okay, it's settled. I'll see you after class."

She gave Kurt directions and they left.

When Chloe got home, she didn't know what to do with herself. Maybe she should just be honest with Kurt. After all, what harm could it do? She really cared for Meghan. It wasn't as if she'd be taking care of her all that much longer anyway.

She stood in the middle of her living room and looked over at the computer. She had forgotten about the disk her boss had given her. Messages blinked on her answering machine, but she was afraid of who they were from.

Taking a deep breath, she pushed the play button, hoping not to hear Andrew's voice. She hadn't heard from him since that scene at the restaurant. A nagging feeling about that whole thing still lingered. Seeing him talking to Sherry didn't have to mean anything. Luckily there were no unnerving messages. She returned the calls and then felt more like herself. Taking the disk out of her purse, she slid it into the computer and spent time checking out the problems before she called it a night.

She awoke the next morning with a smile on her face that caused her to laugh out loud. The dream she had actually had Meghan in it, almost like the baby she had reached for in other dreams.

Heading into the shower, she knew the dream was because she'd be spending the day with Meghan as well as her sister and niece.

A couple of hours later Kurt arrived with Meghan. Chloe looked out the window when she heard the car and watched father and daughter have a conversation. Her heart sank. Maybe Meghan was changing her mind. Well, there was nothing she could do about it if she did.

After several moments, both car doors opened and Chloe opened her door to greet them.

"Hi Chloe. I'm ready to go. Do you know what movie we're seeing?"

Chloe laughed as she motioned them into the house. "Sorry, I don't know yet. My sister will tell us which one when we meet them." She kept laughing when Meghan plopped herself in the oversize chair by the door. "That's my favorite chair. I think you can see why."

Kurt laughed as well. "I see what you mean."

"Check it out, Dad, there's room for two."

Kurt looked at Chloe and shrugged as he moved to join his daughter. "You have a nice place, Chloe."

"Thanks."

After a few moments, Kurt stood up. "Well, okay you two. Have a good time."

"We will..." Meghan said as she got up and went to check out the large stuffed animals on the love seat.

Chloe walked him to the door. "I'll have her home around six or so if that's okay."

"That's fine. I have to tell you that this is the first time she's stuck to plans like this. I think it's because she trusts you. She doesn't like to spend a long period of time like this away from me, even with people she knows really well."

They walked out onto the porch. "When I saw you two talking in the car, I thought she was changing her mind."

Kurt's face changed. "Actually, we were arguing because she wanted Sherry to go with you guys, but I told her you already had plans with other people."

"Oh, well, if she'd rather do something with Sherry, please don't force her to go with me."

"No, that's not the case. Sherry just showed up at the dance class and Meghan told her what you guys were doing. She really wants to go with you, but she's so used to Sherry being around." He hesitated. "Well, you know what I mean."

Chloe put her hand up. "Hey, I do understand. As long as she really wants to be here, then we'll be fine."

"Okay, then I'll see you tonight." He started walking away and then turned back.

"You know. I can't help feeling that Sherry just might make an appearance." He looked down at the driveway with a perplexed look on his face. Then he looked back at her. "I'm not sure why I told you that." He chuckled. "It sounded more like a warning."

Chloe smiled. "Don't worry, not a problem."

Kurt shrugged. "Oh, well, I don't get it. Anyway, have fun."

"We will."

She watched him drive away as a tingle went up her spine. How could he not get it? He has to know the woman has feelings for him. She didn't know if the tingle was from watching him leave and fighting an unexpected yearning inside, or if it was a warning of what was to come.

Her fun day now clouded over. She knew for sure that Sherry was going to show up and try to do some damage. She needed to figure out how to put the woman at ease. It wasn't her fault that Kurt wasn't interested in her.

They met Sandy and Candace at the movies. As they stood in line, the two girls were trying to decide what they wanted for snacks.

"I can't believe how well they get along," Sandy said.

Chloe laughed. "Time will tell. They are very much alike, I'm afraid. And we know what happens when similar personalities get together."

Sandy nodded. "I know what you mean. So, how are things going?"

Chloe sighed, and making sure Meghan wasn't in earshot, said, "Things are going well. She's a good kid. Misses her mother very much and has put me to the test occasionally, but all in all, no complaints."

They arrived at the snack counter, got their choices and headed to the theater number marked on the tickets.

With the girls ahead of them, Sandy whispered to Chloe.

"Do you think it's been a good enough experience for you to think seriously of adoption?"

Chloe shrugged. "I don't know. It's only been for a short time, but I've learned a lot from you and the rest of the family as well, and I guess I just have to decide to take the plunge."

"Any idea where to start?"

"I've looked into agencies that deal with both domestic and international adoption. There's a lot to understand before I can even begin to decide how I want to proceed, if at all.

The two girls found seats in the front of the theater and Chloe and Sandy decided to let them sit by themselves. They would sit further back. Once settled, Sandy leaned over and still spoke quietly, "I understand that it's important to research all this adoption stuff, but as far as I'm concerned, you'd make a great mom regardless."

Chloe gave her sister a sidelong glance. "Thanks, I appreciate that."

The lights went out and the movie started. Good timing, as tears welled up in Chloe's eyes. Would she really make a great mom to some stranger? Was her sister just being sisterly? Finally focusing on the movie, she relaxed and enjoyed herself. For a kids flick, she found herself laughing a lot. It was a good sound.

When the movie was over, they headed to a park. Until the moment Chloe saw Sherry, she had actually forgotten about her.

Meghan waved and continued to walk toward the swings with Candace.

"Who's that?" Sandy asked.

"That's Sherry."

"Oh, say no more."

Chloe waved as Sherry approached them, and put on her best smile. She introduced the two women and prayed her sister would behave herself. Sandy had told Chloe that the woman was jealous of her being around Kurt, not jealous about her being around Meghan. Chloe wasn't convinced.

"How was the movie?" Sherry asked.

Both women responded at the same time. "Good"

They found a couple of benches to sit on and chatted while the kids played.

About thirty minutes into the relaxing time of general talk, there was a yell and then all three women were running. Meghan had fallen. Candace said they were trying to see how far they could jump off the swing and both hit the ground at the same time, but Meghan fell forward, landing hard on her left hand.

Sherry had gotten to her first and was hugging the child like she was dying. "Are you okay honey?"

Meghan was trying to be brave as her eyes filled with tears. "I, I'm okay… just landed wrong."

Sherry blocked Chloe from trying to see what was going on. "It looks like you may have sprained your wrist, sweetie. I think you should go to the hospital and get it checked out."

Meghan looked at Chloe, but when Chloe went to reach for her, Sherry had the child up on her feet and was leading her to her truck. "I'll take her. You can stay with your sister."

Chloe blinked and gave her sister a look that told her to stay out of it. "Thanks, Sherry, but she's my responsibility, I'll take her."

Sherry stopped and after a dagger filled look at Chloe, turned to Meghan. "Meghan, honey, who do you want to take you to the hospital?"

Chloe heard the intake of breath from her sister. "Sherry..."

Meghan began to cry. Chloe's heart broke as the child looked from one to the other. Chloe would not play tug of war with her. "Okay, Sherry, you take her and I'll call Kurt and meet you at the hospital."

Sherry didn't respond. She got Meghan into the truck and took off.

"Wow," was all Sandy could say.

"Mom, is Meghan going to be okay?"

Sandy ruffled Candace's hair. "Yes, honey. Looks like she sprained her wrist and possibly broke a finger."

"Can we go to the hospital too?"

Chloe answered. "Of course we can."

The three of them walked to Sandy's car. They decided to leave Chloe's at the park. As they got in, Candace said, "I don't like that other lady."

Chloe and Sandy glanced at each other and then they drove off. Kurt was already at the hospital when they arrived.

He came out of the emergency room, looking very pale. Color came into his face when he spotted Chloe. He walked over to the three of them and asked to speak to Chloe alone without bothering with introductions.

Chloe felt a bit sick. To feel so helpless when Meghan got hurt was a reminder of some of the downs a parent would experience. Would she really be up to the test?

Then Kurt broke into her thoughts. "What happened?" he asked, through gritted teeth.

Chloe was taken aback. Didn't Sherry tell him? Or even Meghan herself? She blinked several times. "Ah, she jumped off the swing and fell after she landed."

"Why weren't you watching her?"

"What?"

"You heard me. Why weren't you watching her?"

Chloe's heart was pounding as she glanced over to where her sister was. "I was. I mean, they were on the swings and we were all talking." She swallowed.

"Oh, never mind. I'll talk to you later."

But when he turned to head back into the emergency room, she grabbed his arm, panicked that something more had happened. "How is she?"

She watched him try to control himself. At least he didn't pull away from her. "She'll be fine. Looks like a sprained wrist and index finger. The pinkie is broken."

"Oh, thank God it wasn't worse." She still hadn't let go of his arm. "I'll wait here until everything is taken care of."

He finally pulled away from her. "That won't be necessary. Sherry and I will take care of her from here. I'll see you on Monday."

She watched him walk away, her stomach clenching and tears lurking once again.

Sandy walked over to her. "Are you all right? You don't look so good."

"Let's get out of here." She turned to walk away.

"Is Meghan okay?" Candace asked as she tried to keep up with her mother and aunt.

"Yes, she'll be fine."

They got into the car and drove back to the park. Because of Candace, Chloe kept her thoughts to herself, except for explaining Meghan's injuries. Sandy, knowing her sister well, kept her mouth closed.

When they got to Chloe's car, Candace asked if she could swing for a few more minutes. Sandy let her go so she and Chloe could talk.

"Okay, spill."

Chloe looked at her sister. "He's blaming me."

"What?"

Chloe started crying. "He wanted to know why I wasn't watching her."

"You've got to be kidding me. There were three of us there. Unfortunately, these things happen. He's just a Dad, very upset his child was hurt."

Chloe took a deep, shuttering breath. "I can just imagine what Sherry told him."

"Oh, come on. This is ridiculous. You actually think she said it was your fault?"

Chloe just looked at her and Sandy closed her eyes. "She's that much in love with the man?"

Chloe's heart did a little flip at the mention of love. Wiping her eyes, she started to laugh hysterically, a stress relief laugh. "I guess love does that to you. Something I wouldn't know about."

"Oh, now you're just feeling sorry for yourself."

"Well, how would you feel?"

"Awful, but I wouldn't blame you for what happened."

Chloe took a deep breath. "Well, at least she'll be okay. These things happen to kids, right?"

"Right. And, Chloe, they can happen to all children, no matter who's on watch."

Swallowing back another bout of crying, she nodded. "You're right. But the look on his face when he came out of that room…"

"Was one of anger and relief, and wanting to blame someone. It was a natural reaction for a parent. But I'll tell you something else, Chloe. He had a look of needing comfort, too, and when you stopped him from walking away from you, a calmness came over him."

Chloe frowned and shook her head. "I didn't see it."

"Well, you were under attack and trying to make things right."

Chloe thought for a minute. "I guess you're right."

"Of course I am. Older sisters are always right."

They both laughed and Chloe said, "at least they like to think so."

After hugging each other, Chloe got out of the car and started walking toward her own. She waved good-bye to Candace.

As Sandy got out and started walking toward the swings, she said, "Don't be too hard on yourself, Chloe. Talk to him on Monday and straighten everything out. All will be fine."

"You're right, it will be. After we straighten this out, I'm quitting."

Chapter 5

Chloe returned home exhausted, along with a fried brain and heavy heart. Failure was also mixed somewhere within. What could Sherry have said to Kurt to blame her for what happened? It was an accident. Meghan was taken care of immediately. Chloe would have been the one to take her to the hospital if Sherry hadn't been there.

Plopping in her favorite cushy chair, she mulled over the thought of quitting. She had no choice. Kurt would just have to find someone else to take care of Meghan. She half laughed. He probably already had someone lined up. Maybe she'd be saved the trip to his house on Monday because he'd contact her and fire her before then. Well, so be it. She knew deep down in her heart that he would believe Sherry over her any day. And what about

Meghan? Did the child feel she was neglected and not taken care of?

Closing her eyes and taking deep breaths, she fought for some encouragement. Kids had accidents. Hopefully they weren't serious. But they came with the territory of raising children. She had a strong impulse to call and see if Meghan was okay, but was afraid to hear Kurt's judging voice. Maybe they weren't home yet and she could at least leave a message. *Coward.* Most likely, but at least they'd know she truly cared.

Forcing her leaden legs to get up and walk toward the phone, she held her breath and asked God to giver her strength as she dialed their number. No answer. She put on her best caring sound voice and left a message, then she paced, waiting for a call back. Nothing. Two hours later there was still no call back. Her sister had called to see if there was any news and convinced her to stop worrying. The fact was that they were probably home and Sherry was with them. He most likely wouldn't call back until the morning, if at all.

She also left a message for Patti, inviting her to lunch Sunday so she could fill her in on what had happened.

Chloe went outside to get her mail. There was a letter from one of the adoption agencies that she had contacted. After reading the letter, she researched the organization more on line and then decided she would make an appointment to visit them. After all, once she stopped taking care of Meghan, she'd have more time to pursue it. The next thing she did was write a letter of resignation to Mr. Simpson and then went to bed.

Sunday morning dawned with gray skies and rain showers. When Chloe woke up, she couldn't remember where she was. Another dream. She frowned trying to remember it. It was very hazy and she couldn't figure out what it was about, no matter how she tried. At least she didn't feel badly about it. That in itself was a good thing.

After showering and having breakfast, she toyed with the idea of calling about Meghan again. More frustration caused her to groan out loud. But remembering the look on Kurt's face at the hospital stopped her from making another call. She would just have to bide her time until tomorrow.

The doorbell rang.

When she looked out the window, her heart nearly stopped. Kurt's car was in her driveway. Oh, no. He came to fire her in person? Well, of all the nerve. She worked herself up, ready to tell him off first. But when she opened the door, the words never made it out.

"Hi Chloe. Dad wanted to call first, but I told him you needed to see me and I wanted to surprise you."

Chloe blinked several times and then carefully hugged Megan after taking a quick look at her father. Was that regret in his eyes, along with sheepishness?

"Come in. How are you feeling?"

Meghan sat in the comfy chair and showed Chloe her partial cast. "I'm good. It still hurts, but I can move my other fingers."

Kurt was standing next to the chair. "I hope we didn't disturb you, but she insisted that we surprise you in person instead of returning your call."

"No, not at all. Please sit down." She gestured toward a rocking chair for Kurt. "Can I get you anything? Coffee, juice?"

"Ask her, Dad."

Kurt shifted in the chair and looked at the floor before looking at Chloe. "We are actually on our way out for breakfast, which we always do after church, and wondered if you'd like to join us."

"Please Chloe?" Meghan asked.

How could she say no? Did Kurt have a change of heart? She felt sure he was going to let her go. Maybe he still was, but just not today.

"Ah, sure. Where would you like me to meet you?" No need to tell them she already ate.

Meghan got out of the chair. "Dad will drive us all together." She headed for the door as Kurt stood.

Chloe got her purse and met Kurt at the door. Meghan was already outside getting into the back seat of the car.

"I'm sorry, Chloe. I know the accident wasn't your fault."

Their eyes met and for a moment time froze. Chloe felt as hazy as the illusive dream she couldn't remember. Then, she broke contact. "I'm glad. I feel bad enough as it is."

She walked out in front of him and then waited for him to step out so she could lock the door. He actually lightly touched her back as they walked down the stairs.

At the restaurant, all three of them ordered pancakes with sides of bacon. Meghan had chocolate chip, Kurt had blueberry and Chloe had strawberry.

While they waited for their food, Meghan looked at Chloe and said, "Why didn't you stay at the hospital yesterday?"

She looked at Kurt, at a loss for words. Thank God he responded.

"I told her to go home, honey. She wanted to stay, but I wasn't sure how long you'd be there."

"Yeah, but Sherry stayed the whole time."

Chloe's heart sank as she waited for Kurt to answer again. "Well, Chloe was with other people, and I didn't think it was fair to have them waiting around."

He was a bit flushed after scrambling to come up with an explanation. The waitress walked over and dropped off the various syrups for the pancakes. It was enough of an interruption for him to get normal color back in his face.

Chloe took over. "So, how long do you have to wear that?" She felt a little queasy looking at the colors of the fingers that were injured, but Meghan didn't seem to think it was a big deal.

Both father and daughter filled in the details and then the food arrived. It was good timing since Chloe's thoughts strayed to her own physical injuries.

With no other interruptions and embarrassing questions, they settled down to enjoy a nice breakfast.

Meghan shared the story of the priest saying a special prayer for her recovery when they saw him after mass. Chloe still didn't feel she could say anything about them belonging to the same church. She was afraid they'd invite her to join them and she couldn't explain why she wouldn't, at least not yet.

It was a perfect family picture. Without warning, tears appeared in Chloe's eyes and she blinked them away before anyone could see them. Excusing herself, she went to the ladies room.

Now what was she going to do? She was still so sure he was going to let her go, but everything seemed normal again. Was he just indulging his daughter? Would he still let her go tomorrow? What had changed his mind? Maybe it was as Sandy said; he was just reacting as a scared parent.

Looking in the mirror, she chastised herself. What about Kurt? What kinds of things went through his mind doing all these things without his wife being a part of it? Embarrassment settled within and snapped her out of such selfishness.

Taking a deep breath, she returned to the table to find both Kurt and Meghan getting ready to leave.

"Thanks for coming out with us, Chloe. Dad didn't think you would, but I told him he was being silly. You like us, so why wouldn't you?"

Chloe's heart did a little flip. *You like us.* That was true enough. But what was there not to like?

Meghan talked their ears off on the ride back to Chloe's. "You know, Chloe, the priest at church this morning said that forgiveness and love are priorities."

"Yes, I believe that too."

"Do you go to church?"

Chloe didn't expect that question. "Sometimes."

"We didn't go after Mom died. Just started going back recently. Where do you go?"

"St. Agatha's."

"Really? That's where we go, right Dad?"

"Yes, honey."

"Maybe we can all go together sometime."

Neither Kurt nor Chloe responded and it didn't matter because Meghan went off in a different topic of discussion.

Once they arrived at Chloe's, she dared a look at Kurt quickly before getting out of the car. A sense of relief seemed to be on his face and she knew in that instant that she was not going to be fired. Her own sense of relief was overwhelming.

"See you tomorrow, Chloe," Meghan said as she got out of the back seat and into the front.

"Okay, see you then." She waved good-bye as they drove away, Kurt's eyes still sending her apologies.

She went in to call her sister and the phone rang. Expecting it to be Sandy, she picked it up. It was Andrew. Instinct made her hang up on him. Then she felt guilty. Why was she always feeling guilty about things, especially regarding him?

The phone rang again and she let the machine pick it up.

"Chloe, I know you're there. Please pick up. I want to apologize for the last time we saw each other. Please. Pick up."

Chloe put her hands on her ears. *No, no, no.* She would not pick up the phone no matter how much she wanted to. At least he wasn't leaving messages on her cell phone. In spite of that last scene with Andrew, she still loved the sound of his voice. But it was a deception she would not get caught in again.

She paced back and forth for several moments, talking to herself and anything in the room that would listen. Why was he tormenting her like this?

She finally stopped pacing and looked out the front window. Why wouldn't the man leave her alone? There was a time, even the last dreadful meeting, that she thought they may be able to... to what? Get back together? She groaned and started pacing again.

A sneaky feeling swept through her and she visibly shook. Something wasn't right. She decided to call her mother and tell her what was going on. After more than an hour on the phone, she felt much better. Her mother was very encouraging, but too far away in California. Would she be able to ease a child's fears as her mother could do and help them through the tough times in life, no matter their age?

Children. She loved them and always believed she'd have one or two, but not through adoption, especially adoption as a single parent.

Groaning again, she lectured herself for always thinking that way. Any child deserved a home, no matter where they came from. A longing appeared in her heart and she picked up the information from the adoption agency and read it again. Then she went to the computer to do more research. Even though she may be researching the topic to death, she needed to be sure she was doing it the right way. For the child's sake, she kept telling herself, even though deep down, she still felt unworthy of one.

Taking one step at a time, her heart told her she was doing the right thing, in spite of any reservations she still had.

Thoughts of Meghan suggesting they go to church together kept popping into her mind. Maybe that would be how she would go back to church. Would God forgive her for anger at not being able to have a child? She was grateful for her life and didn't want to be a hypocrite.

After another bit of adoption research, she began to feel a little more confident.

She stretched in her chair and was thinking of preparing lunch, when the doorbell rang. Expecting that it was Patti, she was glad of her timing so they could have lunch together and fill her in on everything.

It was not Patti standing on her porch. It was Andrew.

Her heart shifted, but she made no move to invite him in. Something told her to step outside onto the porch.

"What are you doing here, Andrew?" Andrew put his hands up. "Look, Chloe, I don't blame you for being suspicious, especially after I was such an idiot the last time we got together."

Chloe folded her arms across her chest and leaned against the door jam. She didn't say a word, just watched him fidget.

"Come on, Chloe, I'm sorry."

She sighed. "You said that last time."

"And I meant it." He rubbed his hand through his hair. "Oh, I don't know. You just made me crazy. I finally come to my senses about you and then I couldn't believe you were turning me down. You know I get...."

"Nasty when you don't get your way," she finished for him.

"Yeah." And there was the boyish grin she had come to love. One of the many things she had loved about him. The important word was being *had*. Even though her heart and head were fighting one another, the head was winning. At least by a slight lead.

"Andrew, I'm sorry too, but we can't go back. The damage has been done. I'm trying to move on."

He looked into her eyes with more searching than judgment this time. Her heart skipped a beat.

Oh, God, it might have just evened the war with her head. *No, no, no.*

He blinked and then narrowed his eyes just a bit. "You really don't think we can try again?"

God, he was making this really hard. There was no sign of the Andrew she met at the restaurant. He was like a different person being too different. Ha, the head just pulled out in front of the heart.

Chloe's phone rang but she let it go. Letting out a breath she didn't realize was being held in, she said, "Andrew, I don't know what to say to you. You're very different from the last time we met, but, I… I just don't trust you."

She braced herself for his reaction, but it wasn't what she expected. He actually looked like he was going to cry.

A horn tooted and she looked to see Patti pulling up. The relief at seeing her friend was immense.

Andrew turned as well, but didn't make any move to leave.

As Patti approached the porch, Andrew waved and said hello to her. She greeted him only after looking at Chloe first.

"Well," he said. "I guess I'll be going."

He looked at Chloe. "I hope we can continue this discussion at another time."

Chloe tried to ignore the protective vibes coming from Patti.

"I'll think about it."

He nodded and then turned and headed down the steps. He waved as he drove away.

The girls walked into the house. "What the heck was that about?" Patti asked.

Chloe laughed. "I'm not really sure."

"Oh, no," Patti said.

"What?

"Come on, Chloe. Are you softening toward him?"

Was I? Chloe asked herself.

"I was just thinking of what to have for lunch and he showed up a few minutes before you did. Didn't leave me much room for softening or hardening toward him."

They both went into the kitchen and Patti sat at the table while Chloe got the food together.

"What was he doing here, Chloe?"

"It's the weirdest thing. He's like two different people. He actually seemed more like the old Andrew before the accident." She brought the sandwiches and drinks to the table and sat across from Patti.

"Can you trust that?" Patti asked.

Chloe thought for a second. Could she? Part of her heart still cared for him in spite of all the twists and turns with him lately. "I don't know. He's been such a part of my life and he was so different today from when we met last time, I just don't know. I'm still very confused about the turn of events since the accident."

"Well, as your friend, I'm going to caution you. And maybe I don't have the right, but he hasn't been there for you the way he should have been. You've made a lot of progress and if I'm not mistaken, maybe opening up to other possibilities?"

"What do you mean?"

Patti laughed. "Come on, Chloe, it's me. Are you going to tell me you're not just a little interested in Kurt Simpson?"

Chloe felt her cheeks heat. "Well, let me tell you what happened yesterday and this morning before you came."

She filled her in and watched her mouth drop and eyes widen.

"Oh my God, Chloe. I'm so sorry to hear you went through this. It is obvious that Sherry is interested in Kurt, but I don't believe the feeling is mutual. And for him to give into his daughter's request to surprise you instead of calling you back, gave him time to get his embarrassment under control."

"Wait a minute, I can understand that. Kurt is a nice enough guy, but he's my employer and nothing more. I'll be done with that job in a few weeks. Besides, he's still grieving for his wife."

Patti sighed and took a bite of her sandwich, swallowing without really chewing. "Chloe, I can see it in your eyes. You're interested in the man. And you know what? Good for you. I also feel he's interested in you. Hey, as far as I'm concerned, you don't owe Andrew anything. But I can understand why you're confused."

Chloe smiled. "Well, thank you for that. I know you still don't like Andrew, but I feel something is definitely going on with him. I just can't put my finger on it."

"Well, I agree with that. But if you're trying to move forward with your life, especially thinking of adopting a child, you need to think about what is best for the child. Do you believe that getting back with Andrew is going to make that new life any better?"

Chloe frowned at that. Patti threw a damper on her thoughts as surely as if she had physically thrown water at her. What was she thinking? All thoughts of a child had vanished while she was wrapped up in the latest meeting with Andrew. This was not a good sign for taking a child into her life with him back in it.

Patti interrupted her thoughts. "I can see you still have a lot to mull over. What's going on with the adoption investigations?"

Chloe put her face in her hands. "Oh, Patti, what am I going to do? As soon as I decide to take a step forward, it seems I end up taking three steps back." She stood up and headed out of the kitchen. "Come into the other room and I'll show you the agency I'm researching."

Patti followed her friend, her own frown in place as she wondered how Chloe was going to sort so much emotional stuff out. She was very concerned about Andrew trying to get back into her friend's life. It was time for her to investigate things for herself. She refused to let Andrew undermine everything Chloe had accomplished without him. Chloe may or may not appreciate the interference, but it was her duty as a best friend to look out for her. Feeling like she could finally do something to help Chloe, she put a smile on her face as Chloe handed her the adoption agency brochure and she sat in the comfy chair.

Chloe was very animated as she shared her findings and then looked forward to Patti's response.

"I can see you've thoroughly researched everything. It seems to me you're on the right path."

Chloe sat in the rocking chair beside Patti. "I'm thinking about setting up an appointment to go see them, but that seems like such a scary step. What if this isn't the right path after all? What if I'm just fooling myself into thinking I can do this? It's such a final thing. It's not as if I can just send the kid back if it doesn't work out."

Patty rolled her eyes. "Chloe, I'm sure your sister has told you a number of times that children can drive one crazy at times. Even she has joked about sending them back to the hospital. My mother always used to say that about me, but they don't do it. It's just part of the territory."

Chloe laughed. "You're right. In fact my mother said the same thing to me."

Patti smiled. "Okay, you know it's going to be rocky at times. You have enough love in you for ten kids. What about Meghan? How do you feel about her?"

Thoughts of Meghan made her smile, which in turn got her to thinking about Kurt, which in turn brought Andrew back to mind. Ugh.

Patti rolled her eyes again. "I can see where that question just took you by the changes in your face, one thing at a time. How do you feel about Meghan? Remove both Kurt and Andrew from your crazy head and focus only on her. Do you think you could be with her on a daily basis in spite of any testing she has sent to your way so far?"

Chloe found she could actually answer without hesitation. "Yes. I actually think I love her. To be honest, I'm not looking forward to ending the relationship in a few weeks."

"Well, there you go. If you can focus on what you really and truly want, it should be clear as a bell."

Chloe smiled. "Thanks, Patti. I knew I could count on you to keep me on the straight and narrow."

Pattie rubbed her knuckles on her shoulder, as if polishing them. "Ah, I'll say again, that's what friends are for. Hey listen, I'm not saying that you don't have to deal with both Kurt and Andrew, because I know you have feelings for both of them. The bottom line is, these issues and others will come into your life whether you have a child or not. I know you're trying to do all this on your own, but I don't believe it means you will never have a husband down the road. I truly believe you can do this with or without one."

Tears came to Chloe's eyes. "You're right. I'm just scared of messing up. Messing up my life is one thing, but messing up another life, especially a child who will have only me to depend on, is very scary."

"But, Chloe, it's not as if you'll be doing it alone. You have family and friends who will help you. Your support group goes far and wide. It's true when they say it takes a village to raise a child. Heck, even two parent families need help on occasion. That's just life."

Chloe was so thankful for her friend that she was speechless. And Patti was right.

"What would I do without you?"

Patti smiled. "Beats me."

Chloe laughed. "Okay, I'm going to call tomorrow and set up an appointment. After all, talking about it with an agency will really test me further as to whether I'm heading in the right direction." She frowned. "But it's also true that I have to deal with both Kurt and Andrew. Those two make my head hurt."

"Well, I'm here to help with those guys too."

Chloe smirked. "I'm sure you are."

Before Patti left, they hugged each other and thanked each other for their friendship.

"Hey, Patti, next time we get together, you fill me in on your adventures please."

Patti saluted her, "Aye, aye, captain."

Chloe watched her drive away and suddenly felt both energized and very alone. She decided to go visit her sister, Sandy. It was time to just hang out and not have to worry about all these things she had to deal with. But deep down she knew that her world was about to spin in a different direction.

Refusing to think anymore about it, she headed out, looking forward to being Auntie Chloe, a role she knew she was good at.

Tomorrow will be another challenge for her.

Chapter 6

Monday morning brought a lightness of heart to Chloe as she awoke feeling invigorated for the first time in a long time. The previous afternoon spent as Auntie Chloe soothed her weary soul. Spending time among people who loved her unconditionally helped to put things into perspective. Talking with both Patti and her sister helped as well. She knew Kurt and Andrew had to be dealt with eventually, but her goal now was to visit the adoption agency.

She called the agency for an appointment before going over to Kurt's. The woman at the agency asked a few preliminary questions and then set the time for Thursday morning at ten. Another weight was lifted off her shoulders when she hung up the phone. She did a few more things around the house and then headed to Kurt's.

Meghan seemed a little subdued when she came home from school, but it was mostly because she was uncomfortable with the cast. Instead of being cranky, she asked Chloe to sit with her and watch TV. Chloe felt comfortable with the child sitting so close to her and put her arm around her. Then it hit her. Meghan must be missing her mother at a time like this. Nobody can replace a mother, and yet, Meghan must feel she could receive comfort from Chloe. It was a good sign for a woman thinking of taking on a stranger's life. Her heart melted as Meghan cuddled closer.

Before she could dwell on dissecting feelings, Kurt came home. He was early and when he walked into the room, Chloe's heart fluttered. For an instant she pretended the scene was her family. It was a scene that forced her to admit for a split second that she didn't want to adopt a child alone. But just as quickly the moment passed.

"Hi Dad."

"Hi Ladies. How are you feeling, Meghan?"

"Okay."

Meghan didn't budge from where she was sitting, so Kurt sat across from them.

"How was school?"

"Okay."

Chloe didn't budge either, knowing Meghan still hadn't gotten enough "mothering", so to speak.

"How does your hand feel today?"

Meghan leaned closer to Chloe. "It really hurt at school, but its better now."

Kurt and Chloe looked at each other with a moment of understanding that almost broke Chloe's heart.

"How about I order in for dinner tonight?" Kurt asked.

Meghan vaguely nodded.

"How about I cook something?" Chloe suggested.

Meghan turned her head to look at her. "Like what?"

She shrugged. "What would you like?"

Meghan thought for a moment. "Spaghetti."

Once again, Chloe and Kurt's eyes met and Chloe said, "I'll go and gather what we need."

Meghan snuggled closer. "Not yet. Dad, aren't you home early?"

"Yes, I wanted to check on you."

"You could have called. I'm fine."

Kurt smiled. "I can see that. Tell you what. I'll go see that we have everything Chloe needs."

"Okay."

As if having Kurt there made the loving cocoon complete for Meghan, in a short time she was asleep.

Chloe slowly pulled away and guided Meghan down to lie straight and put a pillow under her head. Finding an afghan on a chair, she covered her and then went to see Kurt in the kitchen.

He was leaning against the counter with his face in his hands. When he looked up at her, there were tears in his eyes and Chloe could not help herself as she walked over and gave him a hug.

They stayed in the embrace for what seemed an eternity when Chloe pulled away and walked to one of the cupboards.

"Thanks."

She smiled at him. "My pleasure. I'm sure it's been tough on you since this happened."

He could only nod.

Chloe could see he was still upset, so she tried to lighten things up a bit. "Okay, I think I can find my way around the kitchen after these few weeks." Not expecting a reply, she reached with shaking hands to open the cupboard where she remembered the pasta was stored. Gathering pans and jarred sauce, she put water in one pot to boil. He was still standing there, looking at the floor.

Chloe opened the freezer and found frozen meatballs along with frozen garlic bread. Hey, whatever it took, frozen or homemade, that wasn't the issue here. Meghan still needed comfort, and from the looks of him, so did Kurt. Oh, God, it was so easy to pretend the situation was real. This scene was way too comfortable once again, but Chloe did what she was beginning to do so often now. Take care of others. She used to do that a lot before the accident, but since then she had focused on herself. Suddenly, she felt a little more confident on taking on a child of her own. These roller coaster feelings of being incapable one minute and then positive the next, will either be going to her undoing or give her the strength she needed.

Regardless, she was beginning to see that she was truly healing enough to switch the focus from herself to someone else.

Kurt finally cleared his throat and moved away from the counter. "I see you have everything under control. I think I'll take a shower before dinner." He stopped when he got to the doorway. "Meghan is awfully quiet."

She looked at him, seeing such weariness that she wanted to hug him again. "She's sleeping."

He smiled roguishly. "I can see why. I know I would too in the same loving and caring circumstances."

He left before she blushed. Remembering what she was doing took a second. The water was about to boil with the sauce that was in the pan. God, her brain was suddenly mush. Taking a deep breath, she continued to re-focus.

When she took the garlic bread out to get it ready to go into the oven, she also noticed a package of break to bake chocolate chip cookies in the freezer and decided to make them as well. The smell of baking cookies would be enough to comfort anyone in need.

Just as the cookies were coming out of the oven, Meghan came into the room.

"Hi Chloe, I thought you left."

Chloe laughed. "What, and not eat spaghetti with you? How do you feel?"

"Better." Meghan walked over to Chloe and gave her a hug. Then she reached for one of the cookies.

"Careful, they're hot."

Kurt had arrived just after Meghan, but stayed outside the room watching.

He couldn't stop thinking about Chloe when he was in the shower. That hug was wonderful. And watching her with his daughter now was even more wonderful. She didn't even tell Meghan that the cookie would spoil her dinner. He sighed. Only two weeks left and she'd be gone. After his initial reaction at the hospital, he almost thought of letting her go, but now he knew that was ridiculous. Accidents happened to kids all the time. He was lucky they hadn't been any worse with Meghan. He also couldn't just dismiss how nice things were with Chloe around. His other inclinations to try to keep her in his life were growing stronger again.

Meghan turned and saw him standing there.

"Hey, Dad, look. Chloe made chocolate chip cookies, too."

He walked all the way into the kitchen. "I can see and smell that." But when he went to take one, Chloe slapped his hand. "You'll spoil your dinner."

Meghan giggled as she finished the last bite of hers.

Kurt scowled. "Okay, squirt, go wash up for dinner."

She left the kitchen, still laughing.

Chloe had just drained the pasta and turned to see Kurt walk toward her with a glint in his eye. Before she knew what he was about, he leaned in and kissed her. "Thank you for all you've done for us."

He stepped back just as Meghan returned. "I'm starving. Everything smells so good." She seemed to be back to her old self. "Dad, why do you look funny?"

Both he and Chloe flushed a bit. "I tried to steal a cookie again, and she wouldn't let me."

Chloe had returned to the oven to remove the garlic bread, hoping her heart and blood pressure would calm down before she was asked the same question.

In a blur, the rest of the food was organized and put on the table. Chloe had lost her appetite, but Meghan and Kurt sure found theirs.

Meghan gabbed through the whole meal and was obviously over her "comfort" need.

When the meal was finished, they tackled the cookies. Meghan still bragged about how Chloe let her eat one before dinner and not Kurt.

Kurt could only laugh and catch Chloe's eye.

"I'll clean up tonight," Kurt said. "But soon enough, squirt, you can help one handed."

"I can do it now, Dad." She picked up her plate and moved it to the sink and then came back for Chloe's. "See?"

"Well," Chloe said, "It looks like you two have everything under control. I'm going to head home."

"Thanks, Chloe," Meghan said.

"I'll walk you out," Kurt replied.

"Oh, that's not necessary."

Kurt chuckled. "I figured you'd say that. I need to talk to you about Thursday."

Chloe blinked and looked directly at him, then turned and walked away. "What about Thursday?"

"Meghan has a half day at school and a doctor's appointment in the morning, so she won't be going at all. Since I was supposed to take the whole day off anyway, I was wondering if you'd like to still come over and the three of us could do something."

"Um, actually, Thursday isn't a good day for me. I have some appointments of my own."

"Oh."

"What kind of appointments?" Meghan asked as she appeared next to her father.

"Meghan, don't be rude. Chloe's life away from us is her business."

Meghan shrugged. "I know. But she knows where we're going."

Chloe smiled. "It's okay. I just have some personal stuff to do, nothing exciting."

She turned to walk away, feeling Kurt's eyes on her.

"See you tomorrow, Chloe." Meghan called.

"See you then, Meghan. Take care of that hand." She turned to wave as she got in the car.

"I will."

"Dad, can I play some x-box?"

"One handed?"

"Why not?"

He looked at Chloe, rolled his eyes and shrugged. "Okay, you can try."

As she drove away, she saw Kurt standing in the doorway watching her. Part of her wanted to go back and bare her soul to him, and the other part of her couldn't get away from there fast enough.

Wow, what had happened? She went from purpose oriented to mush brain in one afternoon. And worse, she had actually contemplated giving up the adoption agency appointment to spend the day with Kurt and Meghan. Correction, spend the time with Kurt. She couldn't deny her attraction to the man anymore. The hug and kiss, although shared in a common thankful atmosphere, held potential for other things to happen. Honesty forced her to admit she craved that attention now.

She returned home and worked more on the computer program her boss had given her. The adoption brochure was sitting next to the computer. Looking at it, she knew she still wanted to go to the appointment. Thoughts of Kurt would have to take a back seat for now. At least she was feeling like a normal woman again.

The next couple of days were back to normal. Meghan was her old self and for that matter so was Kurt. There seemed to be a silent truce between the adults not to be alone together.

Thursday morning arrived and before Chloe went to the adoption agency, she had a physical therapy appointment. Once that torture was done, she left the building and as she headed to her car, Kurt and Meghan were getting out of theirs.

"Chloe, what are you doing here?" Meghan asked.

"Oh, I had a doctor's appointment."

"Did you see my doctor? Doctor Ruben?"

"No, sweetie, I saw someone else. So, this is where your appointment is, eh?"

"Yep. This thing may come off and maybe just a bandage will be put on."

"Oh, well, I hope that's what happens then. Sorry, but I've got another place to be. Good luck."

She smiled at Kurt who she could tell had a few questions for her, but he just waved when she walked away.

"Hey Dad. Do you think Chloe is sick?"

"I don't know. She might have had just a regular check up."

"That's true. I hope she's okay. I really like Chloe."

Me, too, Kurt thought. Me too.

Chloe was more nervous than she thought as she sat in the waiting room of the adoption agency.

An hour later she was back in her car marveling at the whole new world that had been opened up to her. She was both hesitant and excited. The only thing she didn't have doubts about was money.

After the accident, she had felt as if everything had been torn from her. So much could change in a split second. She ended up talking to the adoption lady about the accident in more detail than she ever shared with any stranger. That is, the details she could remember, which weren't many. The kind of details she wanted to share with Kurt. *Where did that come from?*

After that cozy afternoon with Kurt and Meghan earlier in the week, Chloe had been off balance. She knew better than to think it was because of a kiss or a hug. She truly liked the man. He was so different from Andrew and yet Andrew still had a place in her heart. Maybe she should just have a talk with Andrew, a real talk and tell him what she wanted and maybe... *Maybe what?*

On the other hand, maybe she could find an opportunity to talk to Kurt about the same things and then see how the two reacted. He had said he'd be there to listen. She believed he meant what he said. And there was the crux. She believed in Kurt, but still had her doubts about Andrew. But Andrew had been the love of her life. Or so she had thought. Wasn't love supposed to conquer all? In good times and in bad...

She frowned. What if the accident had happened after they were married? Would Andrew have divorced her because she couldn't have children? A chill ran through her. Is that what would have happened?

For some inexplicable reason, she felt a strong urge to contact Andrew. It was the kind of thing that had to be done, regardless of whether it was right or wrong.

She got home and put the adoption agency packet on her desk, then called Andrew, since he worked from home a lot.

A laughing woman answered the phone.

"Ah, is Andrew there?" Chloe asked, caught off guard.

"Yes, he is. Who's calling?"

That voice sounded familiar. "It's Chloe," she managed to get out.

"Oh, hold on. Hey Andrew, its Chloe."

A lot of whispering went on before Andrew got on the line.

"Hey, Chloe. What's up?"

Good question, Chloe thought. Why did she do this? She finally realized the woman's voice belonged to Sherry. A sinking feeling came over her as she thought about the two of them talking at the restaurant that one night.

"Um, sorry, Andrew, I can see this is a bad time."

"No, not at all, Chloe. What's going on?"

"Well, I was thinking about getting together, if you still wanted to." God, she felt like an idiot.

"Sure. That would be great. I was afraid you wouldn't want to after seeing you the other day. When would you like to meet?"

"Well, since it looks like you're busy now, how about tomorrow night?"

"You mean you can meet me now?"

She half laughed. "Not if you have company, Andrew."

"Sherry's not company," he practically sneered. "Besides she's just leaving."

There was just a hint of the old and mean Andrew in that statement. Obviously Sherry didn't like the idea, considering the intense whispering she could hear through the phone.

"Okay. If you want to come now, why don't we meet at Mulligan's in twenty minutes?"

"Sounds good. I'll see you there."

Chloe hung up the phone. What was she doing, and more importantly, what was Sherry doing at Andrew's? Well, she wasn't going to dwell on it. She needed to be frank with Andrew and move on with her life, one way or the other.

But there was that sixth sense that something wasn't right. And she couldn't help feeling that Sherry definitely had something to do with it.

Andrew was already there when she arrived. He had a corner booth already. Standing when she came to the table, he grasped her arm and gave her a kiss on the cheek.

Chloe's first reaction was to pull away, but then she smelled his cologne and was transported back to happier times. She still wasn't sure what she was looking for with this encounter, but it felt right.

They ordered drinks and an appetizer.

"I'm so glad you called, Chloe. I was running out of ideas about how to get you to talk to me again. I'm so sorry for everything."

"Listen, Andrew, I have some questions I need to ask you and I hope you'll be honest with me."

He leaned back in the booth, waved his arms wide and said, "fire away."

"If the accident happened after we got married, would you have left me because I couldn't have children?"

He blinked and opened his mouth to speak, but nothing came out. She could tell he was trying to find the right answer, not necessarily the true answer. That's just how well she knew him.

Then he leaned forward and grabbed her tightly folded hands, holding them gently. "There was a time when my answer would have been, yes, Chloe. But after all this time and realizing how much I still love you, I don't know how I could have turned away from you as I have."

Now it was Chloe's turn to be quiet. It was not the answer she had expected. If he had said, yes, then she could move on sooner. But now she was confused again.

Slowly pulling her hands away from his warm grasp, she took a deep breath. "Okay, question two. I'm in the process of pursuing single adoption because I want a child. Since you have no desire to raise someone else's, why would you still want to get together with me knowing how strongly we disagree on this subject?"

He narrowed his eyes at her and she knew she'd hit a nerve. When he reached for her hands again, she pulled them away. He sat back.

"I don't know what to say, Chloe. I've tried to think of this adoption stuff that's so important to you, but I still have a problem with someone else's child being raised as my own."

He stared at her, as if looking for something in her face. "Can I ask you a question?"

"Sure," she replied quietly, half afraid of what he was going to say.

"Now that you've spent time with someone else's child, do you truly believe you could love a stranger?"

Chloe smiled. "You know, Andrew, you were once a stranger and I agreed to marry you."

"Just answer the question." He gave her a sincere smile, which again brought back good memories. But she couldn't bring herself to trust it.

"I love Meghan very much. And as much as she's not mine, I could see a future with someone like her. Every child needs love, whether blood or not."

He studied her again. "So you really are just using her to see if you can do it yourself?"

She actually blushed. He had said the same thing the last time they had met, but it sounded so much crueler then.

She sighed. "Yes, I needed to see if it worked with a child other than my nieces and nephews. It was part of my therapy to get back on my feet since you weren't a part of my life anymore."

He frowned. "I really did hurt you, didn't I?"

"I don't know how you could ever have thought otherwise," she responded quietly. As much as she could feel her shoulders lightening, a deep sadness had over taken her. She spilled it all to him, but couldn't see how it was going to help in the end, after all. His sincerity only went so far. As much as she wanted to believe otherwise, he truly wasn't the one for her.

"Hey, Andrew," a familiar voice said.

Chloe looked up to see Sherry, and…Kurt. Now she felt totally exposed with Kurt standing there, studying her as Andrew had.

After introductions, Sherry and Kurt moved on to a different room, arm and arm. Chloe didn't know that her heart could sink any further than it was at that moment. And that told her a lot about her feelings for Kurt.

Two weeks. Did she have the stamina to look at him for two more weeks? Nothing had really changed except that he saw her here with Andrew. Something niggled at her, but she couldn't figure it out.

She looked at Andrew who was watching her intently. Too intently, like he was expecting something. Smug. That was the look he was trying to hide. She cleared her throat. "Can I ask you another question?"

"Sure."

"How do you know Sherry?"

He lost the smug look and shrugged. "I met her at a party a friend of mine had. After we split up, he was trying to help me meet new people."

She stared at him. "Does it bother you that she's with Kurt?"

He blinked but didn't skip a beat. "Not at all, why, does it bother you that she's with him?"

Chloe tried to hide her blush, but the glint in his eyes, told her he knew. "No, I already know she likes him. She's also very involved with Meghan."

"And that doesn't bother you?"

Chloe frowned. "Why would it bother me?"

"Chloe, Chloe. It's me, sweetheart. I'm not stupid." He frowned. "Well, maybe I am because of what a heel I've been to you. He's probably the only other non-medical person you've been around in awhile, so I would think it was natural for you to care about the man. Especially someone who lost his wife."

She took a deep breath and tried to control her frustration at all his subtle jabs. "You're right. I can finally feel and care again, which is all I wanted out of this whole thing. And I think he's still missing his wife very much. Hopefully Sherry will fill that void eventually."

Chloe wanted to slap the satisfied look on his face. But he kept his cruel words at bay. "I'm sorry, Chloe. But I think you've been good for the man and his child, based on what Sherry has told me.

Maybe you've helped him with Sherry. From what I know, she's been pining for him for a long time. Guess he's just getting around to seeing her in a different light."

She smiled at him sadly. "Well, like I said, I'm glad to be accomplishing something these days."

Andrew's look tugged at her heart. "Listen, Chloe. If I try to reconcile with the fact of not being able to have a biological child with you and think about this adoption stuff, will you at least let me try to see you again?"

Was this guy nuts? He just set her up to make her face certain things and now he wanted to continue where they'd left off? The niggled feeling was very strong. Maybe if she agreed to his suggestion, she would eventually find out what he was up to.

"Okay, Andrew. Let me think about it." And when he reached for her hands again, she smiled and didn't take them away.

Across the room, Sherry had made sure they sat where Kurt could see the couple. She knew exactly what part of the plan Andrew was at just by watching Kurt's face. The man could not stop looking in that direction. When the final frown caused him to look down at the table, she knew she had won, at least this round.

Chapter 7

Back at home after the meeting at Mulligan's, Chloe invited Patti over to fill her in on the obvious set up at the restaurant. Then she told her what she was up to as she worked on the computer.

Patti just stared at her. "Are you nuts? You can't do this. Unless you really have given up on Kurt and are starting to trust Andrew again."

Chloe continued to search on the computer while Patti hovered by her shoulder.

"Patti, please. I'll admit that spending the time with him on my terms was very different. And I know it was a set up, especially when Sherry showed up with Kurt, but I feel it's necessary for me to do this, if only to get some self-respect back."

Patti shook her head. "I don't know about this. It sounds as if you're setting yourself up for a big let down again."

"I really don't know if there is anything that will let me down like Andrew did after the accident."

"What about Kurt?"

"There is no Kurt. He's my employer and a man who, even if he doesn't realize it, has shown me that I have feelings. Feelings that may not be returned, but they are there none the less."

Patti picked up the latest adoption packet. "And what about all this? Is this going to happen or not?"

Chloe sighed. "I haven't decided yet, but I'm leaning toward doing it. And doing it alone. The meeting went well the other day and I'm going to a group meeting they have twice a month for people looking to adopt. Andrew will never agree and if for some reason he changes his mind, I'll be very suspicious."

"Not that I'm defending the guy, but why would he have such a change of heart?"

Chloe didn't answer at first. "I'm not sure, but I think there's something he's not telling me. Although I can't imagine what it is."

"Did he say he loves you?"

"Yes, and that he wants to try to work it out, including thinking about the adoption process." Of course, she wouldn't tell her friend how often he referred to the adoption subject as *stuff*.

Patti groaned and started pacing. "You're driving me crazy. Why bother with getting back at him? It's obvious he's up to no good with Sherry. Why would either one bother to set you and Kurt up? They must sense something between the two of you and are trying to stop it. Didn't you already tell me that you didn't think Kurt returned Sherry's attentions?"

"Yes, but I don't know everything about them, and maybe Kurt just hasn't faced those feelings for her."

"Or maybe he truly doesn't have any for her and has them for you."

Chloe got off her own chair and started to pace as well. "I think you're the one driving me crazy. Ugh. I take care of his daughter. And, okay, we've had a few "moments", but that's all. He doesn't know about anything going on with me except my computer job."

"Then why don't you tell him."

"Tell him what?"

"Tell him about the accident, about Andrew, and about the possible adoption."

Chloe cringed. How many times had she wanted to do just that? "For what purpose? The man isn't going to care about all this."

"You won't know until you tell him."

"But I don't see why I should burden him with stuff when I'll be out of his life in two weeks. How many times do I have to tell you that?"

Patti stopped pacing, which in turn caused Chloe to stop. The two friends looked at each other and started laughing.

"Why are we practically yelling at each other?" Chloe asked.

Patti sat down on the sofa. "Beats me."

Chloe plopped down beside her. "Okay, I'll be honest with you. I've wanted to tell him so many times. In fact he's offered to listen if I want to talk. But I can't share all this stuff with someone who…"

"Turns you to mush?" Patti asked.

Chloe didn't answer. She closed her eyes and thought of the hug and kiss they shared.

"Chloe, I realize you're healing and taking control of your life. I just don't want you to get so carried away in the other direction that you fall harder than you already did. If you have feelings for Kurt, you need to deal with them and not focus so much on Andrew. I know you want to get back at him and frankly it's a good sign to a point. But I think you need to slow down a bit."

Suddenly, Chloe felt very tired, and for no reason started to cry. Patti cried too and put her arm around her. The two friends had been through a lot since the accident.

After several moments, both calmed down.

"Well, wasn't that fun," Patti said.

Chloe laughed. "Yeah, what a pair we make."

"Listen, Patti, you're right. I do need to slow down. I'm not sure how much I should tell Kurt, even if I decide to tell him anything. To be honest, the next two weeks are going to feel like a month in some ways and too short in other ways. I'm not looking forward to not seeing them anymore."

The phone rang and Chloe blew her nose one more time before answering it.

When she faced Patti again, she looked confused.

"What's the matter?"

"That was Kurt. He said he didn't need me tomorrow and that he'd see me on Monday."

Patti shrugged. "So. Hasn't he done that before on Fridays?"

"Yes, but this time his voice seemed different, like he wanted to say something else."

"I'm telling you, Chloe, the man has feelings for you. If you don't do something soon, Sherry's plan is going to work and you and Kurt are going to be left out in the cold."

Chloe snorted. "If Sherry's plan works, I don't think that Kurt will be left out in the cold." And that bothered Chloe more than she wanted to admit. Eventually the man would cave in to the woman. Wouldn't he?

Patti eventually left with a promise from Chloe that she wouldn't do anything drastic. She wasn't seeing Andrew again until the middle of next week. She made it clear who was calling the shots this time.

Once Patti was gone, Chloe started thinking more about her struggle with God and decided to research some faith sites and other people's struggles. She truly believed she'd be back to church at some point, but knew certain things within her heart and soul had to be healed and encouragement had to be stronger.

After reading some more serious situations than hers on the computer, she felt guilty about her feelings, even though her struggles were legitimate. Every individual situation had to be dealt with. Trust in God needs to be rebuilt. To be honest with herself, she was making some good progress even though it didn't take much to make her fall back to crushing torture over her loss of being able to have a child. On the other hand, she was still grateful for being alive and a deep part of her still believed that God had something special coming her way, in spite of her loss.

Yawning several times finally made her go to bed and she ended up sleeping for almost nine hours. The baby dream appeared again, but this time, the baby didn't float away. It stayed within her grasp even though she couldn't bring it any closer. She tried to interpret it as a good omen that she was closing in on a final decision about adopting.

Thoughts of the call from Kurt started to intrude. If her life was none of his concern, why did he sound like it was a punishment for her not to go there today?

She was coming down from all the adrenalin from the previous day. No wonder she slept so long. She went to her computer and worked on the program again, this time finishing it. She would bring it to the office on Monday morning. Since she slept so late, the day was just about over by the time she finished working. Weariness assailed her again and she didn't bother to fight it. After puttering around the house and doing some cleaning, she was back in bed by nine o'clock.

Now up and screaming at two am. The accident. Her heart was beating out of her chest and sweat poured off her. Realizing where she was and finally taking some deep breaths, she calmed down but also started weeping.

Until this moment, she couldn't remember the accident details. They were only vague shadows with an occasional detail here and there. Now that she could remember more details, she didn't want to. She was afraid to go back to sleep. Oh, God. What was she going to do? Shivering, she got up and went to make some hot cocoa. She was frozen. She was scared. Not only were more accident details clear in her mind now, but some memories of the pain in the beginning was very real at this moment. She flexed her hand and bent her left leg just to be sure they weren't injured again. She put one hand on her stomach and groaned out loud. Tears formed again. She would truly never have a child of her own. Andrew. The thought of him telling her he couldn't marry her and why, turned the tears into anger. All of it was way too much to bear. Kurt. She sure could use a hug from him right now.

On impulse she walked to the phone and dialed his number. Not caring what time it was or that she may wake Meghan as well, she listened while the phone rang a second time. He picked up on the third ring and she couldn't say a word. After saying hello three times, he hung up. For all she knew, he was cursing whoever woke him up. But it had been worth it just to hear his voice. She went back to bed with that warm feeling, very glad she called him. Hoping that it would be enough to keep away any more nightmares.

****

Kurt was wide awake. The caller ID was in the other room, but he didn't feel like getting up to check it. It was probably a wrong number anyway. But there was something about the silence at the other end of the phone that bothered him. He clicked on the TV and set the sleep timer again.

The next morning when he checked the ID, his heart skipped a beat. Why would Chloe call him at that hour? She must have dialed wrong.

"Dad, can we go to breakfast?"

"Not today. Sherry is bringing us breakfast."

"Dad?"

"What, Meghan?"

"Why is Sherry always here? Isn't Chloe going to take care of me anymore?"

Kurt looked at his daughter. "Of course, honey. She'll be here tomorrow."

"Good, 'cause I miss her."

Kurt closed his eyes as Meghan left the room. He missed Chloe, too. But if she was getting back with that guy, there was no sense in thinking about the silly dreams he had about a possible future with her. He wasn't stupid. Sherry was up to her old tricks again. But if someone special was in Chloe's life, he had no right to interfere.

The doorbell rang and Sherry practically danced into the house.

She gave Kurt a kiss on the cheek, and put the food down on the table. "Have I got news for you."

****

Chloe awoke to no new nightmares. But the new accident memories came rushing back to her. She called her mother and talked it out. Once again she felt better. She would have to put it into focus as best she could. She had way too much on her plate.

After hanging up with her mother, she remembered calling Kurt in the middle of the night. She didn't know if he had caller ID, but if he did, he'd either call or ignore it.

She decided to focus on the adoption application. Regardless of whatever was going on in her healing process, she wanted a child. And this was her only option. It took a long time to find a baby in the United States, so she could apply for one and continue to heal and get ready for the call, even if it came years down the road. If she had to, she'd look into a foreign adoption that could come sooner than local, but wasn't sure she wanted to do that.

It took awhile for her to fill out the paperwork. She was very meticulous and went over her answers many times. She felt a great sense of accomplishment when she was done. Then she decided to take a good look at her home and how she would get it ready for a child.

A slight tingle of excitement started to develop as she chose which of the two guest bedrooms she would turn into a baby's room. She'd have to start getting some books and reading up on things. She wanted to learn as much as she could. Everything needed to be perfect for her child.

Sunday flew by without any new emotional upheavals. She had made lists for everything: baby furniture, clothing, diapers, and whatever else she could think of. Her sister and mother were already emailing her suggestions. She also had to be aware that she may not get an infant. A one or two year old was hard to get as well, but she didn't want one much older than that.

By the end of the day she was starting to feel more encouragement. Thoughts of faith challenges she read online helped her to see more and more how lucky she truly was. Heading to bed, she hoped that any dreams would be good ones and not scary. Thoughts had popped in during the day regarding memories of the accident. Even though she felt strongly about contacting her therapist, she wanted to wait until the next scheduled appointment so she could work things out on her own.

Monday morning she brought the computer disk to the office and picked up more work. Monday afternoon she headed to Kurt's. She was very nervous and couldn't shake it.

There was a note that said Kurt would be home around six. That was it, nothing else.

Meghan arrived home and gave Chloe a big hug. "I've missed you, Chloe. How come you couldn't come on Friday?"

Chloe blinked. Now she knew something was up since it was Kurt's idea for her not to come. "Sorry, Meghan, I had some last minute stuff to do. How's the hand doing?"

"Great. See, I have an ace bandage on it now and can use it more."

"Good news, honey. Do you have any homework?"

"No. Can we go to the fair that's in town?"

"Oh, I don't know. I'm not sure your father would want you to go, especially without him."

"Well, Sherry was going to take me this week without him."

"Oh."

"Can you call and ask him?"

"Ah, I really don't want to bother him at work for something like this."

"Please?"

Chloe's heart sank, but she called him anyway. He was very short and to the point with her, but gave the okay for them to go for a little while.

They went and had a great time. But as they were getting ready to leave there was an accident on the highway that was going to put them home later than six. Chloe called the office and got Sherry who said that Kurt was on a call. After a hesitation she explained the problem to Sherry and asked her to tell Kurt.

Since they could see the accident from the fair grounds, they got a bite to eat and watched until the traffic started to move again. The fair wasn't far from the house, but the delay put them back home around seven thirty.

They walked in the house giggling like two little kids. Both of them walked into the kitchen where Kurt was on the phone. He hung up and leaned back against the counter.

"Hey, Dad. We had a good time. Thanks for letting us go."

"Glad to hear it, honey, go get ready for your shower." His gaze never left Chloe's as he spoke to Meghan.

"Dad?"

"What."

"Is something wrong?"

"No, just go."

"Okay. Bye Chloe."

"Bye, sweetie."

Chloe wanted to run away. She couldn't read into the scowl on Kurt's face, but she could only assume it had to do with the other night, or maybe it was the call to him in the middle of the night.

She frowned. "What's the matter?"

"I don't know where to begin, Chloe, but for starters, where have you been?"

Her frown deepened. "At the fair. There was…"

"I know you were at the fair. Why weren't you home by six?"

"There was an accident on the highway…"

"You couldn't call?"

She blinked, not knowing what to say. Numbness began to seep into her. He was definitely holding back his temper.

"I did call. I gave Sherry the information to give to you."

He actually sneered at her and her blood ran cold.

"You know. I didn't realize you had a problem with Sherry until just now. Why would you lie about that?"

Chloe was getting angry. "What time did you leave the office?"

"It doesn't matter."

"Oh, yes it does. I called at five fifteen when I knew we couldn't get back on time."

Kurt took a deep breath. Shaking his head, he looked at her with weary eyes that crushed her heart.

After several heartbreakingly long moments, he said, "Chloe, I don't think I'll need your services any longer."

Chloe caught her breath. Did he really say what she heard? "But…"

"No buts. I've been sick with worry."

"Unnecessary worry since I called. I think you better talk to Sherry."

"Leave her out of this."

"I don't understand you, Kurt. I would never hurt you or Meghan for any reason."

"You don't understand," he said, quietly.

"Kurt, I love Meghan like she was my own."

"But she's not your daughter, she's mine."

Time stood still. As her heart slowly broke into tiny pieces, she realized what had transpired.

"I'll go get the final check for you." He turned and walked away.

Chloe stood shell-shocked. He had to be kidding. One part of her wanted to follow him and tell him a thing or two. She also wanted to kill Andrew and Sherry. Their hands were in this whole thing. The other part wanted to get out of there. She chose part two.

Kurt walked back into an empty kitchen as he heard her drive off. His hands shaking, he wondered what the heck he was doing. Even though he had a hard time believing what he had found out, his priority was protecting his daughter.

"Dad, I'm ready."

"Coming, sweetie."

He brought the check back into his home office and stood like a lost soul. He should have known better than to think he was ready to give his heart to someone again. But as he put the check in the desk drawer, he sighed. At least he still had a heart. He felt the cracking of it right down to his toes.

"Daaaad…"

"Coming," and he headed up the stairs trying not to think of the devastation he saw on Chloe's face.

Chapter 8

Chloe pulled into a shopping center parking lot to calm herself down. She punched the steering wheel a few times and forced several deep breaths into her emotionally battered body. Now she really had both physical and mental pain going on. As if she needed anymore of both in her life.

Instead of being dragged under by the disappointment of everything at the moment, she found her mind racing in a million different directions. After several minutes of deep breathing and mind racing, she finally calmed down. Way down.

The delayed shaking started and she wanted to throw up. Both came under control in a few minutes. She leaned her head back and closed her eyes, willing herself not to fall apart. What kind of parent would she be if she fell apart every time something shocked or disappointed her?

And then she knew. This was all a test. The accident, Andrew's betrayal and her climb out of a hole filled with pain. The struggle to get her life back had been harder than she could imagine. And then there was Kurt. Even though the thought of him now made her angry, he made her feel again. And Meghan. A bond had grown between the two and she knew for sure that one could happen with any child. The thought of not seeing Meghan again was what finally brought on the tears.

Then she felt close to God again. Finally realized he had guided her through all this crap to prepare her for a new life adventure. The thoughts of not being able to have her own child was still hard to wrap her head around, but her heart was pulsing stronger with more open intentions to reach out with love.

She passed the test. Now she needed to take care of herself and get on with her life. Alone for now.

It began raining and she started to laugh. Here she was in a shopping mall parking lot making important decisions about life. Not at a beach or mountain setting, or sitting in front of a roaring fire. A mall parking lot with life moving around her, not even aware she was there.

She started the car and drove home. When she arrived, it was pouring. She got out of the car, but instead of running up the steps, she stood with her face toward the sky. The pelting felt like a massage bringing her relaxation and invigoration at the same time. She sneezed, laughed and then ran up the steps. No sense in getting ill. But as she entered her house, she felt renewed both inside and out. She loved her home, loved what she could offer another person; be that a man or a child. Or both?

She jumped in the shower and then threw on some comfortable clothes. Starting a fire, she curled up in the comfy chair and started to read one of the child rearing books she picked up. In a matter of minutes she was asleep.

*****

Meghan came downstairs to find her father sitting in the den alone with no television on or music playing.

"Dad?"

"Yeah."

"Can I have a snack?"

"Sure."

He heard his daughter leave the room, but didn't move from the chair. He should probably go join her, but he truly wanted to be alone. Emotions warring with each other, he went from anger to sympathy and back so many times that even he couldn't keep up.

Meghan came back in and nearly made him jump when she appeared at his side, holding out a cookie and glass of milk to him.

"What's the matter, Dad?"

"Nothing, honey," he said, reaching for the milk and cookie. "Thanks for bringing this to me."

"You're welcome. Can I put the TV on?"

"Sure."

She put the television on and went to get her snack. Kurt watched her return and plop on the sofa, nearly spilling her glass of milk. He almost reprimanded her, but held back.

Visions of her cuddling against Chloe came to mind and he almost groaned aloud. How could he be so dense? He must be truly lonely if he was bringing to mind comfortable scenes. Scenes that he wanted back in his life. But if Chloe was only using them as a test of her parenting abilities, as Sherry had said, she must be contemplating the same kind of scenes, right? He knew she would never hurt Meghan, but Sherry made it sound almost diabolical in her news about what she found out. And he'd known Sherry a lot longer than Chloe.

Meghan's laughter brought him out of his thoughts for a minute. She was so much more open since Chloe came into their lives. Heck, even he was more alive. But now he felt like a heel. Regrets at letting Chloe go, assailed him. But he couldn't tolerate lying and he knew that she and Meghan were getting close. So? So, what? Was she planning on kidnapping his daughter? Of course she wasn't. She would have been moving on in another week or so anyway. *But you didn't want to end the relationship there.*

"Dad, did you see that?"

"No."

"But you're looking at the TV."

"Sorry, squirt, my mind is elsewhere."

She rolled her eyes and looked back at the show.

He focused on the show too and waited for a commercial. When it came on, he asked her to tell him what they did at the fair. She was so animated about the fun time she had that she missed watching the rest of the show. He tried to find a way of asking her if Chloe had called him.

He didn't have to worry because she told him about it when she came to the end of everything they did.

"Then Chloe said there was an accident. We could see it from the fair. But you know that Dad, 'cause she called you to say we'd be late. Then we got something to eat and left when the road was clear."

"Well, it sounds like you had a really nice time."

"We did. I like Chloe, Dad. She's fun. I can't wait to see her again."

Kurt's heart sank. He really had painted himself into a corner. Could Sherry have lied? He knew she had feelings for him, but would she go that far? Sighing, he faced his daughter. Regardless of who was lying, she had to know that Chloe wouldn't be coming back. He also didn't complain to the company about Chloe. Didn't want to cause her any problems.

"Ah, honey, I've got something to tell you."

Her expectant look made him waiver a bit but he trudged on. "Chloe won't be coming again. I decided to take some time off, so we won't need her."

Meghan blinked several times. "You mean while you're off? She'll be back after, right?"

"No."

"Why not?"

"Well, you knew this was only temporary and so did she. I'm just taking time off sooner than I planned."

"But, why didn't she say something to me? She didn't say good-bye."

He watched his daughter's face crumble as his heart broke inside. "I'm sorry, honey, I'm sure she would have if she could."

"But why couldn't she?"

How could he tell her the real reason? He couldn't. He watched the tears form.

"Come here, baby." He reached out to her, but she didn't budge.

"It's just like mommy, but Chloe isn't dead. I don't want her to go away. Can't we see her sometime?"

"I don't think so, honey."

"Did I do something wrong?"

"No, of course not. I told you I just changed my mind." I'm the one who did something wrong, he said to himself.

"Come and let me give you a hug."

Meghan shook her head and then ran out of the room crying.

Kurt got up to go after her, but stopped. What could he say? He didn't need to say anything; he just needed to be with her. She wasn't like this when her mother died, but she was older now. God help him.

He found Meghan curled up on the bed, little hiccups shaking her body. He didn't ask a question, he just picked her up and held her. She cried all over again. Neither one spoke and after several minutes, she quieted and then finally fell asleep.

Kurt laid his daughter down, kissed her cheek and covered her. Then he went into his room and cried a few tears of his own.

****

Chloe awoke a couple of hours later and saw that it was just before ten. She got up and went to call Patti.

"He fired me."

"What? Why?"

"Well, in so many or not so many words, he accused me of lying to him. And then felt it necessary to remind me that Meghan wasn't my daughter."

"Oh my God. I'm coming over."

Chloe laughed. "No, I'm fine, really. I just wanted you to know what was going on."

"Tell me what happened."

Chloe filled her in. "So here I am. Sorry I didn't call you earlier, but I dozed off for awhile and I also called for a favor."

"Sure, anything."

"Would you go with me to the group adoption meeting next Tuesday?"

"It would be my pleasure."

"Good, because I plan on calling Andrew's bluff when I see him Thursday. He's not going to want to go with me when I ask him, so I need a backup plan."

"No problem. Are you sure you still want to meet with him?"

Chloe sighed. "Yes. I hope this will be the last time I have to see him."

"I'm really sorry about Kurt, Chloe. Are you sure you don't want to tell him off or anything? I'll do it for you if you like."

"No. I'm still in shock right now. I'm mainly concerned about Meghan. What lie is he going to tell her? She's got to think I've run out on her. I feel just awful about not being able to say good-bye."

Patti sighed through the phone. "Well, you sure have been on a rollercoaster ride, but I'm concerned about your heart, Chloe. I know you're still struggling with feelings for Andrew, but I need you to be honest with yourself on how you truly feel about Kurt, present anger aside, of course."

Chloe didn't answer at first. "I don't know. But it doesn't matter."

"Of course it matters. I'm your best friend, and I'm telling you that you've fallen for the guy."

Chloe managed a half attempt at a laugh. "Yeah, yeah. Like I said, it doesn't matter."

"Sure. Why don't you call me tomorrow when the reality of it hits, okay?"

"You're such a know-it-all."

"Of course I am. Now go get some rest."

"Yes ma'am. Good night"

Chloe hung up the phone and went to the computer to do some work. After fifteen minutes of doing more staring than working, she went to bed.

The next morning she awoke with no dream memories and a mission on her mind. She began to clean out the one guest bedroom that would be good for a child. She needed to clean that room out anyway, so even if she didn't get a child, the room could be used for any number of things.

As she stood there contemplating, she realized that just the thought of cleaning that room for anything but a child was incomprehensible. Driven by an unknown force that she didn't want to think about.

Thoughts of Kurt and Meghan kept trying to intrude, but she pushed them aside as best she could. In reality though, the harder she worked, the angrier she became.

After taking a lunch break she checked in with her office and then began to go over the furniture list she had made. The rest of the day went along uneventful.

Wednesday was when what had happened hit her. She was angry and disappointed. It shouldn't bother her that Kurt believed Sherry over her, but it did. It was, however, second in line to not saying bye to Meghan.

Did Meghan miss her as much as she did her? Did Kurt?

Wednesday morning Chloe went to see her therapist and actually walked away feeling stronger. She wouldn't see the woman again for a month. After doing a few errands and grabbing lunch, she returned home around one thirty.

Her heart stopped when she turned into the driveway. Meghan was sitting on her porch. Alone.

Several thoughts went through her head at once, none of them good.

As she walked toward the porch, Meghan looked okay, if not a little guilty.

"Hi, Meghan, what are you doing here?"

"I wanted to see you."

Chloe looked around for any sign of another person, or car.

"How did you get here?"

She shrugged. "I took the bus with Shelly who lives a couple of streets away from you. Then I walked over."

"At this time of day?"

"We had half a day today."

"Well, come on in. We better call your father so he knows where you are."

"He thinks I'm at Shelly's. He sent a note to school that said I could take the bus to her house."

Chloe was thinking how young Meghan was to be playing these types of games, but for now she wouldn't bring it up.

When they entered the house, Meghan sat in the comfy chair. "Can I get you a snack? Or didn't you have lunch?"

"I ate a Shelly's before I came here."

Chloe sat across from Meghan waiting to see what else the child would say. When she fidgeted without speaking, Chloe started in.

"I'm a little concerned that you're here by yourself, and that you lied to your father."

When tears started to form in Meghan's eyes, Chloe's heart contracted. "Listen, honey, I'm not mad at you, but you have to understand the safety issues with what you've done. Did you walk here from Shelly's alone?"

She shook her head no. "Shelly's mother knows I'm here. Shelly is in your back yard waiting for me."

Chloe let out a breath. "Well, the first thing you're going to do is call your father. I'll let Shelly in while you do so. And, Meghan, you can call me anytime you want, and visit, but only if your father says it's okay."

"He won't."

"Won't what?"

"Let me call or visit, that's why I did it this way."

Chloe's heart sank. He was still angry with her. But why take it out on his daughter? What would she do in a situation like this with her own child? There was no way of knowing the answer to that.

Hopefully she wouldn't come across a situation like this.

She stood up and grabbed the phone. "Here, call your father and tell him where you are and that you're going back to Shelly's after having a snack."

"Do I really have to?" Tears beckoned again.

"Yes."

"I'm going to go let Shelly in while you call." She didn't want to hear any part of the conversation she had with her father.

Chloe introduced herself to Shelly and brought the girl into the kitchen. Meghan entered a minute later, teary eyed.

"Everything okay?" Shelly asked.

"He's mad at me, but says we'll talk about it later."

Chloe was busy getting snacks and drinks out on the table. She sat at the table with the girls and took a cookie. "Well, these aren't as good as homemade, but I hope you'll like them."

Both girls grabbed a cookie and Meghan said to Chloe, "The one's you made at my house were really good."

"My mother makes them with nuts," Shelly said.

155

"I don't like nuts in cookies," Meghan replied.

"I do, depending on what kind of nut," Chloe said.

After several minutes of talking about cookies and their ingredients, Chloe started to clean up. "I think you girls should head back to Shelly's."

"I can't," Meghan said.

"Why not?" Shelly and Chloe asked.

"My Dad's picking me up here. He'll drop you off at home."

Chloe's heart stopped. What was going on? She wasn't ready to see him yet after what happened.

She needn't have worried. All he did was toot the horn when he arrived.

She walked the girls to the door and opened it, but didn't show herself.

"It was nice meeting you, Shelly."

"It was nice meeting you, too."

Meghan threw her arms around Chloe. "I'm going to miss you, Chloe."

"I'll miss you too, sweetie. Now, remember, don't do this again, okay?"

"I won't."

"And take care of your Dad, okay?"

Meghan gave her an odd look and nodded, then went out the door, followed by Shelly.

It took all she had not to look out the door or window, but she closed the door and walked right back into the kitchen, listening for the car to leave. Once she heard it she relaxed. Well, that was done. At least she felt better about seeing Meghan again. But her heart really wanted to see her father. *Do not go there.*

Chloe stood in the middle of her kitchen looking out the window. Even though Meghan did a very foolish thing, at least she hadn't done it alone. She was actually quite clever, which was very scary.

Well, that was none of her concern any longer. She went back to work in the guest bedroom and this time took measurements so she'd know what furniture would fit where. She definitely knew she wanted a rocker type chair in the room so she could comfort a child in the middle of the night when he or she had nightmares, or was ill. Even though she didn't know the age she would get, hopefully the child would be of an age to need that kind of comfort.

She was looking forward to the adoption meeting next week, whether or not Andrew attended. She really didn't think he would. Why he was pretending, she didn't know but intended to find out.

She met with him the next night at the local mall. She wanted to do some furniture window shopping and figured they could meet at the food court.

He was already there when she arrived, looking so much like the old Andrew that her heart twisted.

"Hi, Chloe," He said rather sheepishly.

"Hi."

She took a seat at the small bistro table.

"Do you want something to eat or drink?" He asked.

"No thanks, this shouldn't take long."

Andrew actually looked disappointed. "So, have you thought about us at all?"

Chloe swallowed and tried to mentally calm her heart down. "I have, and to tell you the truth Andrew, I don't think I can make you a part of my life again."

His brow furrowed and he sincerely looked hurt. "But I thought after the last time I saw you that there was a chance."

Chloe shook her head. "I'm not giving up on adopting a child and that's final. We can't have a relationship when one of us doesn't agree with that."

A spark of hope lit his eyes. "Well, to be honest, Chloe, I've done a lot of thinking and I think that maybe I could consider adoption after all."

Chloe blinked and then searched his eyes for any deception. There wasn't any and that scared her even more. Had he gotten so good that she couldn't see through him any longer?

"What do you mean, maybe?"

He shrugged. "I mean, I'm not so against it as I was before."

"But what changed your mind?"

"You."

She was at a loss for words and her heart was beginning to tumble all over again.

He reached for her hands and she didn't pull back. She desperately wanted to believe him, but at the same time, something was very different.

He squeezed her hands. "Listen, I know I've been more than a jerk to you but I'm begging you for another chance."

She pulled her hands free and sighed. "Andrew. I don't know what to believe with you."

"I know, I know," he said, contritely. "Anything Chloe. Anything you want me to do, I'll do."

Chloe wanted to scream at him - *why didn't you say those words to me after the accident?* But she held back. Her next question would be the test.

Still looking into his eyes for deception, she gave in. "Okay. Come with me next week to a group adoption meeting and we'll see what happens." *Gotcha.*

"Okay, I will. Tell me when and where and I'll be there."

Chloe blinked again and he laughed. "I can see you don't believe me and I guess I don't blame you. But you'll see, Chloe, you will."

Chloe gave him the information and still looked for deception. "Well, I've got some shopping to do."

Andrew chuckled, "Well it must not be for yourself because I know how much you hate to shop."

Chloe's heart skipped a beat. He was so much like the old Andrew that it hurt. Not being able to help herself, she smiled. "True, actually I'm going to start looking at children's furniture." There was another opportunity for his true self to show.

As they both stood up, Andrew said, "Would you mind if I joined you? I guess I need to start getting used to the thought of these things too." And then he winked and she melted just a little bit.

He suddenly looked around. "Ah, you weren't going to do this with someone else, were you?"

"No, why?"

"Well, I wasn't sure if your employer and his daughter would be showing up."

Interesting, Chloe thought. There was actually a hint of the meaner Andrew in that question, but she let it go. Did she dare to think that he might be jealous?

"No, well I don't know if they'd come to this mall at this time, but no. I'm done with that job anyway."

"You are?"

"Yes. I told you it was only for a few weeks."

She could see Andrew thinking and didn't want to go there, so she started walking. "Let's check out that store over there first."

As they walked into the store, Andrew lightly touched her back to have her go in first and a shiver went through her. For now she would ignore it.

A few hours later and with more ideas for a kid's room than she could imagine, they finally parted ways in the parking lot.

Andrew walked her to her car, still trying to get her to go out with him on the weekend. But she held her ground and would only see him at the adoption meeting the following week.

When he leaned in to kiss her, she allowed it. It wasn't a peck on the cheek. It wasn't unpleasant either. But unfortunately, it did nothing to her that Kurt's had and that sent her reeling emotions all over the place once again as she drove home.

Chapter 9

Meghan and her father sat in the living room.

"Talk to me, Meghan. Why did you do it?

"I wanted to see Chloe."

Kurt was trying to stay calm, but he'd been so scared that he just wanted to shake her.

Meghan's lower lip trembled. "I - I'm sorry."

Kurt took a deep breath. "Listen honey; wanting to see Chloe is one thing. But you lied to me and you know I can't tolerate lying."

"I know," she replied, still trying not to cry.

He ran a hand through his hair. "I can't tell you how scary it is to think of what could have happened to you. I also know I have to punish you, but have not decided in what way."

Meghan looked at him with such sad eyes that his heart broke. "You already have punished me, Daddy."

Several moments passed before he could ask, "How?"

"By not letting me see Chloe anymore."

Kurt couldn't be more shocked. Is that how his daughter truly felt? God, he was in over his head. "Honey, I told you that Chloe's job of taking care of you was just over early".

"I know, but you said I couldn't see her anymore."

"That wasn't to punish you. It's just that she has her own life and I didn't think we should bother her." Guilt ate at him as the excuses came out of his mouth.

"But I thought we might be able to see her once in awhile, Dad. Don't you want to?"

More than he wanted to admit. But his daughter didn't know all the details and he didn't know how to take back the words he said to Chloe when they parted. Her shocked and pain filled face still haunted him.

Trying to take a lighter note, he leaned forward. "Listen, sweetie, I'm sure Chloe has better things to do than hang out with us. She worked for me and now she doesn't. I think we have to leave her alone."

Meghan looked at the floor with a frown. "Who's going to take care of me?"

"I am, silly. I told you I'm taking my vacation early."

"So nobody's going to come here to watch me?"

"Nope."

The doorbell rang and Sherry's voice could be heard. "Anybody home?"

Kurt responded. "We're in here. Meet you in the kitchen."

Kurt was taken back by the look Meghan was giving him. "Why is she here?"

He stood up. "She brought us dinner."

"Why?"

He half laughed. "Because I asked her to, squirt. Come on, go get cleaned up and we'll talk more later."

He watched his daughter get up and leave the room. Something was still on her mind. And one person was on his mind as he headed to the kitchen. Chloe. Thoughts of the night she made spaghetti and cookies washed over him. How many times had he thought about that situation and wished there had been more times like it? Too many to count as he made his way into the kitchen where he knew Sherry would not conjure up any of those feelings.

Meghan walked into the kitchen just as Sherry finished putting the Chinese take out on the table.

"Hi, honey, I got your favorite Chinese meat."

Meghan didn't respond as she sat down. Instead, she looked at her father and said, "Dad, Sherry works for you and we see her a lot."

Kurt and Sherry exchanged looks. "Yes, but she still works for me, honey, and she and her family helped us out a lot. She's like family." He cringed inwardly, hoping Sherry didn't take the comment to heart. By the bright smile she gave him, he realized he'd failed. But she responded to Meghan anyway.

"You and your father are very important to me. I like taking care of you both."

Meghan shrugged. "Chloe liked taking care of us too."

"Meghan," her father warned.

Meghan put food in her mouth, not looking at her father.

Sherry responded. "Of course she did, sweetie, but her job is done now."

Meghan looked at her. "Does that mean if you stop working for my father, we won't see you anymore?"

Kurt could see that Sherry took it the wrong way because she responded the opposite of what his daughter was implying, the little scamp.

Sherry reached over and put her hand on Meghan's arm. "Oh, no, Meghan. I will always care about you whether I work for your father or not."

He watched his daughter pull her arm away and glare at him. He knew what was coming, but the frown told him she was honestly confused.

"Then I don't understand why I can't see Chloe once in awhile."

Kurt's initial response was tempered by the moistness in her eyes. A quick glance at Sherry showed him a different set of eyes.

He raised his hands in surrender. "Okay, enough. I'd like to eat in peace." He dug into his food but had lost his appetite. He didn't want to look at either one of them. After several moments of oppressive silence he sighed.

"Okay. This is the last thing I'm going to say about this, Meghan. Chloe is gone and that's the end of it. Please just finish your dinner."

"I'm not hungry," she said with a pout.

"Fine. Then you can leave the table."

"Fine." She pushed out of her chair and ran from the room, yelling back, "I hate you."

Bulls-eye. Could his heart break anymore? And when Sherry patted him on the shoulder, he fully understood how his daughter felt when she removed her arm from Sherry's touch earlier.

*****

Tuesday arrived quicker than expected and Chloe was nervous about the adoption meeting. She didn't expect Andrew to show up, so her nervousness was more about her doubts that she could go through with this.

"Relax, will ya," Patti said as she drove them to the meeting.

"Easy for you to say. You're not the one planning on taking a small life into your hands."

"True," Patti responded, "but I'm planning on being a very involved designated aunt. Provided of course, Andrew doesn't object."

"I'm not making these plans with Andrew. He's not going to show up."

Patti didn't answer right away but then responded. "Well, my friend, unless I'm mistaken, I think Andrew is two cars behind us."

Chloe fought not to turn around. Instead, she pulled down the visor and pretended to look in the mirror checking her eye. He was behind them.

"Oh, God."

"Maybe it's just a coincidence."

"Maybe."

Ten minutes later, both cars turned into the parking lot. Chloe was beside herself. She was actually disappointed that he had shown up. She didn't move out of the car right away.

"Chloe, you invited him. Now just get out and see what happens."

He was just arriving at her side of the car in time to open the door and help her out. He had that glint in his eye that sent shivers down her spine and not the nice kind. By the time she stood next to him, the glint was gone.

The three of them walked in and found seats. They were amazed at how many people were there.

Two hours later, Chloe was more confident than scared. There was a lot to adopting. But in the end, those who shared their experiences showed her that it was well worth the effort.

She tried not to watch Andrew's reaction to certain things that were said, but he seemed to be as much in awe as Chloe and Patti were.

As they walked out, Andrew said, "Um, do you think I could give you a ride home, Chloe? That way we can discuss things."

He was so hopeful that she didn't have the heart to say no.

"Will you mind?" She asked Patti.

"No, of course not. I'll talk to you tomorrow."

"Thanks for coming with me."

"My pleasure. Heck, if I don't find Mr. Right soon, I may just have to look into adoption myself as well."

Chloe slapped her on the shoulder and laughed as she let Andrew lead her to his car. She may have laughed at Patti, but she knew Patti would make a wonderful mother.

The first few minutes of the drive were quiet. Finally Andrew spoke.

"There's a lot involved with this adoption stuff."

"Yes, there is."

Silence again.

"And you really want to pursue someone else's kid?"

Chloe was wondering how long it would take for Andrew to show his true self again.

"Yes, and I thought you said you had changed your mind about it."

Andrew shrugged. "Yeah, well, I have, but it still doesn't feel right. I guess when you have no choice in the matter…"

Chloe clenched her teeth and then decided not to hold back anything she was feeling. "Yeah, especially when that choice is taken from you so cruelly."

Andrew quietly answered, "yeah" and Chloe relaxed a bit. Maybe he was truly coming around. Then he said, "life is full of surprises", a little more sarcastic than expected.

"C'mon, Andrew, this is not something we can take lightly. Life's surprises can be devastating. I sure never wanted the ones I've gotten this past year or so."

Andrew looked sideways at Chloe. "I wasn't talking about you."

Chloe's mouth opened and closed. What was that about?

"Ah, what I mean is, what happened to you affected me as well. They were surprises that affected both of us."

Chloe watched him slip between two different personalities again. Warning bells rang and she was tired of trying to figure him out. Kurt. The urge to talk to Kurt was so strong at that moment that she could cry.

They pulled up in front of Chloe's and Chloe wouldn't get out of the car just yet.

"Andrew, we need to be sure about this. YOU need to be sure about this."

He blew an impatient breath out and tapped the steering wheel with his fingers. "Look, Chloe. I told you I want you back and if this is what it will take, then we'll do it."

Chloe's heart tumbled. This was too important a step to take without feeling secure in the decision. As she looked at her lap, Andrew reached over and covered her hand. Nothing. She actually felt nothing. What was she doing?

"Chloe, I'm sorry. It's just so much to take in. A year ago, we were happy and making plans and now look where we are."

Chloe looked him in the eye. "Just where are we, Andrew?"

He shrugged the annoying shrug that drove her nuts. "We're pretty much where we want to be, but without the possibility of having our own children together. Of course, now I'm considering adoption as well, so I guess that's different."

Chloe studied him and then a brilliant thought came into her confused head. "Listen, Andrew. Maybe this adoption thing is too much to handle right now. You're right; there truly is a lot to think about. I think I still need more time to think about this adoption situation as well as along with the possibility of us. Maybe even the possibility of us without children."

Andrew released her hand and sat back. "Really? But I thought children were the priority for you?"

"Well, I think they still are, but I'm also still realizing just how much work they will be. Maybe I just don't want to deal with it at all. Maybe I'd like my life just fine without them. Hmmm, I never really considered this possibility. I could just continue to be a reliable aunt and not have the full responsibility of a kid all the time. Heck, maybe the accident did me a favor, after all."

She wanted to laugh at the appalled look on his face. "Chloe, what are you saying? Are you feeling okay?"

She laughed. "Andrew, I haven't felt this good in a long time." She got out of the car and leaned back in. "Thanks for the ride. I'll be in touch."

"But, what about us?"

Chloe was surprised at the panic on his face. She gave him one of his own shrugs. "Don't know. I need to think. Call me in a few days if you want. Right now I need to be alone."

She walked up her steps and into the house, shaking so bad that she barely plopped into the chair before falling into it.

The car hadn't started up again, so she knew he was still there. Would he follow her in?

Finally, the car started and he drove away.

She wanted to talk to Kurt. She should have talked to him when he offered. But would it have made any difference? He didn't even acknowledge her when he picked up his wayward daughter. How was Meghan doing? Her heart broke a little more every time she thought about the child. Any child. She would definitely pursue the adoption and without Andrew. She couldn't afford to play his games, and she was sure he was playing a game. She was also sure she didn't want to find out what it was.

She went on line and emailed her psychologist, hoping to set an appointment tomorrow if possible. She also researched some information learned at the meeting.

The stories shared by people who adopted were so encouraging.

Heading to bed she hoped there would be good dreams verse the struggle dreams she was having less and less of. Gratefully, it took her no time to sleep and dreams were very few and not memorable.

The next day, she had a strong desire to go to the park and observe any kids that were there. She hadn't been back to that park since Meghan's accident. Memories of that day and the hospital scene with Kurt played over and over in her mind.

She received an email from her psychologist that she could see her late in the day.

Chloe thought the timing would be good since she was determined to go to the park and whatever she observed would help her explain how she felt.

Once there, she found a bench far enough away that it wouldn't look like she was intruding on any kids that were there. Only pre-school age kids were there at this hour of the day. She watched as kids played, fell, cried and laughed, and had diapers changed and ate. The mother's looked a little harried at times, but still enjoyed spending time with their children. She could definitely see herself in this scene.

So involved with the scene before her, she didn't notice the approach of people from her left.

"Hi Chloe."

She turned to see Kurt and Meghan, both a little hesitant to approach. Heck, why did she always have to make people feel comfortable when she wasn't?

Putting a bright smile on her face, she said, "Hey you two. What's up?"

Meghan looked at her father and he fumbled a bit with his words. "We're just coming from a doctor's appointment and decided to stop by the park for awhile."

"Why are you here?" Meghan asked.

"Just enjoying the day," she lied. How could she tell them why she was really there?

"Can I go on the swings, Dad? Please? I'll be careful."

"Okay, I'll push you."

"No, I can do it. You stay and watch me with Chloe."

She was bounding off before either Kurt or Chloe could respond. Kurt stood there watching her go as if she were going miles away.

"You can have a seat, Kurt, I'm not going to bite."

The relief on his face was comical as he faced her and then stepped toward her to sit down. "Well, I wouldn't blame you if you did. It's what I deserve."

Well. That's not what Chloe was expecting to hear and she wasn't going to make it easy on him, even if she deserved a little something as well. She waited.

"I don't know how to say I'm sorry for what I said to you when you left that night."

Part of her wanted to say it was okay and to comfort him, but she would not do it. She never meant him or Meghan harm. Couldn't he see that?

"I miss you," he said so quietly she almost didn't hear him. Did he really say it? She glanced at him and could see in his eyes that he said something meaningful and maybe even hopeful?

"I miss you guys, too." Coward that she was, she couldn't quite bring herself to say she missed *him*.

He smirked and his eyes took on a deeper color. "Come on, Chloe. I said I miss *you*."

Searching his eyes again, she lost control of the flush overtaking her neck and face. "Oh, all right. I miss you too."

"Now that wasn't so hard, was it?"

"More than you know." She smiled and they both reached for each other's hand. Her world tilted and they both chuckled like little kids exploring a crush.

"Tell me your secrets, Chloe."

Her smile vanished and she tried to take her hand away, but he wouldn't let go.

"Please, Chloe. I feel bad about everything, but I feel you're hiding something and I guess I just felt…"

Chloe pulled her hand away. "That I was trying to take your daughter away? Gee, I wonder where you got that idea from?"

It was his turn to flush. "No, of course not. It's just that, well, I think I was jealous."

She looked at him. Was he kidding?

"I knew she was attached to you. Well, she's so young and vulnerable. And losing her mother just makes it easier for her to get close…"

"To the wrong people?" Chloe folded her arms across her chest.

He sighed. "Yes." He pushed his hand through his hair. "Why is this so hard for me?"

Chloe raised a brow.

"You're not making this easy for me, are you?"

"Should I?"

Kurt paused for a minute. "Yes, I think you should. I've apologized and am trying to let you know how I feel about you and I was such an idiot. You on the other hand, are not alleviating any of my concerns on why I have these suspicions about you."

Chloe frowned. It was now or never. But if she told him, would he understand or would it only confirm what he thought? She needed to bite the bullet or she'd be playing games like Andrew.

"Okay. I'm tired of feeling guilty all the time, so I'll share some stuff with you."

Kurt leaned back on the bench. "Chloe, I've always felt there was something going on, but didn't want to be nosey."

"Appreciate that Kurt. To be honest, I wanted to share things with you several times. I just didn't want to take up your time."

Taking a deep breath, she started.

"Over a year ago I was in a car accident. At the time, I was engaged to Andrew."

A clear look of understanding came over Kurt's face as the Andrew puzzle, along with what Sherry told him, finally came together as Chloe continued.

"Thankfully I'm still alive, but unfortunately my injuries were severe enough that I cannot have children." A feeling of relief came over her as she shared the information. Tears also started to appear.

Kurt put his arm around her shoulder and gave her a handkerchief.

Chloe slowly leaned into him and she wiped her eyes and then sat up again.

"Thank you."

Kurt took the cloth back. "You're welcome."

Kurt tilted his head. "Wow, I'd never know you had such serious injuries. You look great Chloe."

"Thanks. It's been a long road."

Kurt sighed. "I understand long roads."

Chloe took his hand. "I'm sure you do. I don't know how you and Meghan, along with the rest of your family and friends, have dealt with your loss."

Kurt looked at Meghan on the swings. "I don't know how we have either. There are times when I still can't accept it. I still have frustrating conversations with God. How could he allow this to happen? Then other times, I'm grateful to still have my life and Meghan."

Chloe nodded. "I hear you. As upset as I've been with God for taking the birth of a child from me, I am grateful to still have my life. The only thing I still can't bring myself to do is go to church."

Kurt nodded again. "I understand that as well, but I had to force myself to put Meghan's life ahead of mine. We go now and then, but still not on a weekly basis."

Chloe looked at Meghan on the swings. "You go to St. Agatha's, right?"

"Yes. Did Meghan mention it?"

"No, just mentioned going to church, but not the name of it since the other day when I attempted to go for the millionth time but didn't, I saw you two going in."

"So you belong to the same one?"

"Yup."

They both started laughing.

Kurt watched Meghan swing as Chloe told him her story. When she was done, he wanted to hold her, but something held him back. When Chloe touched his arm and swore again that she would never do anything to hurt him or Meghan, he didn't pull away, but didn't offer her comfort either. She actually had used them, but no harm had truly been done, except for one thing. She had made him and his daughter fall in love with her. He wanted the truth and now that he had it he wasn't sure what to do with it. It would have been easier to get her out of his life because she was a monster than to want her in it because he loved her.

He also realized that even though she told him about Andrew and the accident, she was still holding something back. Maybe she didn't trust him even though what she shared was pretty depressing. In fact, it was more a factual tale than an emotional one, regardless of the tears that fell. That was what was missing. A person couldn't go through all that without some continued emotion.

Meghan was running toward them. "Dad, I'm hungry."

"Me too, honey. It's getting late anyway."

"Yeah, I have to go as well," Chloe said. She stood up and reached her hand out to Meghan. "It was nice to see you again. How's your hand?"

Meghan flexed it for her. "Dad?"

"It was nice to see you, Chloe. Let's go, Meghan."

"But, Dad…"

Chloe and Kurt stared at each other for a moment before Chloe reached her hand out to him. Did she have to do everything? "Nice seeing you, Kurt. Take care of yourself and the squirt."

Kurt's eyes flashed surprise. "Maybe…"

Chloe shook her head and said "Bye" and went in the opposite direction they had come. Meghan's voice pleading something with her father was the only thing she heard.

When she finally rounded a corner with trees and bushes, she started breathing again and looked through the bushes. They were still standing there talking, Kurt looking in the direction she had gone. Her heart pounded as she thought they were going to follow, but they turned and went to their car and left.

She would not cry. It felt wonderful to talk to him, but she couldn't quite let herself share the grief of her experience and how encouraged she was while taking care of his daughter. She believed that he was glad she practiced with his daughter, even though he didn't say it.

After several moments, she walked back to her car, stopping to swing for a few minutes. If only life was so simple.

Heading to the psychologist was good timing. She only took a few minutes to summarize what she had been going through and how encouraged she was becoming. She actually did most of the talking with the woman nodding her head more than speaking.

The psychologist was very impressed with Chloe's accomplishments and encouraged her to spread out the appointments more as time went on.

Chloe was very encouraged by the woman and could see that eventually in the future she would be done seeing the lady. It is another accomplishment that made her proud.

When she finally returned home, she wished being back on the swing at the park. A bouquet of flowers was waiting on her porch and they weren't from Kurt.

Chapter 10

Chloe's gut reaction when she saw Andrew's name on the flower card was to throw them away. The disappointment she experienced when they weren't from Kurt should tell her something. She wanted Kurt and not Andrew. It was clear as crystal in that one moment but not that it hadn't been earlier in the park. Then anger at Andrew for sending the flowers warred with the disappointment.

As she entered the house, leaving the flowers on the porch, a memory flashed and then slowly, another one. The accident. She was remembering more of it. Her heart sped up and she gulped air as she sat in the living room chair. It was awful with the screeching of truck brakes and honking of a horn. Or was it horns being the crushing noise?

She threw up on the carpet.

Everything came flooding back with the physical pain along with Andrew's rejection. What was truly going on with him now?

How could she even think about taking him back? Hope. Always underlying hope that things would still work out, and a hope that was always buried, but occasionally acknowledged.

She cleaned up the vomit and took a shower, the scene of the accident playing over and over as the cool water tried to soothe her. It couldn't be held back any longer, so she let herself cry her heart out as the water washed away her tears and she howled like a wounded animal.

Exhausted and with tears still lurking, she fought not to call Kurt. Although it felt good to share more with him, she couldn't bring herself to truly share with him how devastated she'd been. Somehow she owed it to him, especially when it was always clear the struggles he had since losing his wife and trying to raise a child alone. Now that she could recall the accident details, the devastation was complete, yet not able to bring her as low as it could if the details were recalled sooner. She had come too far in re-building her life. It must be the only reason she didn't feel like crawling into a hole to die. Closing her eyes, she thanked God for guiding her through all this crap to bring her to an encouraging time. She still asked Him for forgiveness for blaming Him with the loss of her having a child.

After drying off, she knew what to do. She changed her mind about hanging out at home and headed out the door.

When she arrived at Kurt's, no one was home. She laughed. What did she expect?

Her cell phone rang and she laughed again. Most times she never remembered to put the phone on.

"Hey Patti, what's up?"

"Where are you?"

"Sitting in front of Kurt's."

"Ah, ha. I knew you'd come to your senses eventually."

"Yeah, well, no one's home, so don't go getting excited."

"Are you going to wait for him to appear?"

"Probably not, but I'm not sure what I'm going to do. Patti, I remember the accident. Everything."

"Oh, no. Are you okay?"

"I'm better now, but…"

"You went to share all this with Kurt?"

"Yeah."

"Well, that's good to hear because I've got some information for you that should shed some light on why Andrew's been acting the way he has."

"Really? Well it doesn't matter, because I'm done with him. I'm going to focus on the adoption after I've told Kurt everything. I did share some stuff with him at the park today. I decided to observe children for time before I saw my psychologist and he and Meghan showed up after her doctor appointment. Her hand is doing much better."

"That's great to hear, Chloe. Do you think there may be a future with Kurt?"

Chloe laughed, "Please Patti, don't torture me. I've decided to go forward with this adoption on my own with no men, at least now."

As Patti started to respond, Kurt pulled in.

"Sorry to interrupt, Patti; I've got to go, Kurt is pulling in."

"Okay, but call me so I can fill you in."

"Will do."

Taking several deep breaths, Chloe forced herself to get out of the car. Kurt was already walking toward her.

"Chloe?"

She couldn't help herself. She jumped into his arms and let him hold her. He didn't say a word. Just held her as she cried. He only released her when she tried to step away.

Wiping her face, she half laughed. "Thanks. That's not what I had planned."

He smiled. "I can't wait to hear what you had planned."

She laughed again, but before she could tell him why she was there, Sherry pulled in the yard with Meghan.

Her heart sank. Well, what did she expect?

"Sorry Kurt, I'll be on my way."

Kurt's face fell. "What? You can't just leave me hanging."

She glanced at Sherry and Meghan who was waving and yelling her name as they approached.

He reached for her arm. "Please don't go."

"I don't want to interfere." She pulled a tissue from her purse and pretended to sneeze a couple of times so it would cover her red eyes.

"Chloe, there's nothing going on with Sherry and me."

Sherry reached them and stepped close to Kurt as Meghan hugged Chloe. "Why are you here?" she asked.

Kurt answered as he stepped away from Sherry. "She stopped by to visit."

"Isn't it a little late in the day?" Sherry asked.

"No," Kurt replied. "Thanks for bringing her home, Sherry. I'll see you at work tomorrow."

Chloe watched Sherry's face fall as the dismissal hit.

"Bye, Sherry," Meghan said.

"Bye, honey."

"Thanks again, Sherry." Kurt said.

"Anytime. See ya Chloe."

"Bye."

Sherry wasn't even in her car yet when Kurt was escorting Chloe into the house, Meghan chattered up a storm.

"Meghan, would you like some x-box time?"

"Really Dad?"

"Yes."

"Oh, I get it. You want to talk to Chloe alone."

Chloe and Kurt exchanged looks.

Meghan rolled her eyes and left them, humming as she skipped out of the room.

Kurt motioned Chloe into the den. Instead of sitting on the sofa with him, she took the chair across from it, smiling when Kurt raised an eyebrow.

He leaned back on the sofa. "Talk to me, Chloe."

Chloe didn't need to go through what she had already shared with him at the park. But this time, the emotions weren't held back. Even though she didn't cry again, the anger, frustration and despair finally came into the open.

When she was done, she looked at the floor and then over at Kurt. "So, I've decided to pursue this adoption myself and being with your daughter has greatly helped encourage me to consider bringing a stranger into my life forever."

"I love you, Chloe."

Chloe gasped. "Kurt, please, you're only complicating what I need to do with my life."

He smiled. "If you didn't care for me, too, it wouldn't be a complication. Go ahead and pursue the adoption, Chloe. Let me be a part of it."

Chloe frowned. This was not part of her plan. Oh, maybe it was part of a dream, but a fantasy, but not a reality.

"Kurt."

Kurt stood and approached her, causing her to stand as well, but she edged toward the doorway.

She held out her hand to stop him. "Kurt, you're not going to convince me of anything so don't try.

I'm leaving now. I just wanted you to know the truth about everything."

He folded his arms across his chest. "Okay, Chloe. Have it your way for now. But I'm warning you. I'll be patient for only so long. It's time for me to start a new life as well. And I want you in that life."

Why did he have to say such things? She got out of there as fast as she could, barely yelling a good-bye to Meghan.

Kurt watched her go out the door and smiled. Meghan found him and asked what was going on. While looking out the window and watching Chloe drive away, "Well, Sweetie, I think your Dad is in love. What do you think about that?"

When she didn't answer right away, he turned and looked down and saw her frown.

"What is it, honey?"

"Does this mean you don't love mommy anymore?"

He knelt down and put his hands on her shoulders. "Of course not. I will always love your mother."

"So, are you going to marry Sherry?"

"No. Why would you think that?"

She shrugged. "Sherry always says how she likes to take care of us and is always around, so I thought you'd marry her."

It was Kurt's turn to frown. "Well, I guess I can see why you'd think that, but what do you think about Chloe?"

His heart lightened as his daughter's face brightened. "You mean you're going to marry Chloe?"

He wanted to say yes, but in truth could not. He still didn't have Chloe in his life as he wanted. "Well, squirt, I think I might like to, but we'll have to see as time goes on."

She beamed. "I love Chloe too, Dad."

They hugged each other and then Meghan stepped back and looked at her father with a bright face.

"Then I guess you should marry her, Dad."

"Well, I guess we'll just have to convince her then, won't we?"

Father and daughter laughed and gave each other a high five.

*****

Chloe drove straight to Patti's. Kurt loved her. In spite of everything, the crazy man loved her. But could one love someone in such a short time? Why was it that every time she made progress, another curve ball was thrown her way? Granted this was a rather nice curve ball.

Patti greeted her before she got up the stairs. "Well, don't you look awesome, special friend, so come on in and tell me everything."

They sat in the living room. "He loves me."

Patti frowned. "Chloe, Andrew…"

"Not Andrew. Well, of course he said he loves me, but I'm talking about Kurt. He said he loves me and he wants to be part of the adoption process."

Patti's mouth fell open. "What? But I…"

Chloe giggled. "I know. Can you believe it? And the best thing is that he practically kicked Sherry off his property when she tried to get close to him just now."

Patti just looked at her. "You mean just now at his place?"

"Yeah, she showed up with Meghan after I hung up with you."

"Wow."

"I can't tell you how alive I feel right now. But I can't let it distract me. I'm going to apply for the adoption as a single person."

"But how do you feel about Kurt, Chloe? Maybe you two can adopt a child together?" She wiggled her eyes.

Chloe leaned her head back against the sofa and sighed. "Wouldn't that be perfect? But he has a child and even though he seems eager now to be a part of the process with me, it doesn't mean he won't change his mind down the road."

"Chloe. Are you nuts? The man loves you. I think he's serious about being a part of this child's life with you as well as having you for his daughter."

Chloe raised her head and sighed. "We haven't known each other all that long, Patti."

"True, but you both have been through tough times, and those times give a person an edge on what is important in life."

"Yeah, well, getting involved with someone who's gone through a tragedy isn't necessarily the best foundation for building another relationship either."

"You're looking for excuses, Chloe. Do you want the man in your life or not?"

Chloe didn't answer at first. But then she looked at her friend. "I would love to have him in my life, but I don't know that I can trust him."

"Because of Andrew."

"Yes and no. I don't think Kurt is the same type of man as Andrew, but then, I would never have expected Andrew to abandon me as he did. And I don't understand why Andrew is the way he is now."

"I do."

"Oh, right, you have information, don't you?"

Patti paused before sharing the news. "Andrew wants you back because *he* can't have kids."

Chloe blinked. "What?"

Patti nodded. "I did some investigating on my own because I didn't trust him and felt I needed to help you out."

"How did you find that out?"

Patti laughed. "I have my ways. Let's just say that he found out during a recent medical examination. As the story goes, now that he can't have kids of his own, he was safe with you since you couldn't have them either. He wouldn't have to worry about getting involved with someone who wanted *his* kids."

It was Chloe's turn to be speechless. Then she started laughing. "My goodness. No wonder he's been so insistent. Yet, as much as he wanted to get back together and accept the adoption idea, it still wasn't something he truly wanted. He was willing to settle to save face."

"So what are you going to do?"

"Ugh. I don't know. Revenge can be sweet after all, but I'm really not made that way. At least I'm relieved that I had already decided he's out of my life."

"And Kurt can be in it?"

"Pushing, pushing."

Patti laughed.

"In all seriousness, I do need to confront Andrew. I don't think I told you, but he sent me flowers and has been calling."

"Well then, I guess maybe you've come to the end of the Andrew story. It's a matter of how you want to do it."

After several minutes of sharing her accident dream, Chloe left Patti's feeling both exhausted and liberated. How was she going to handle Andrew? Part of her wanted to rub it in so badly, but the other part knew how devastating it was not to be able to have kids. Memories of the conversation when he said he would consider adoption after all, didn't settle well with her. He only wanted her now because he felt no one else would want him. A bit of a change for him since he obviously believed that no one would want her for the same reason. How wrong he was.

After a dreamless and good slept night, Chloe took the official step of starting the adoption process. She was still convinced she would be a single parent, so that's how she approached the process. Once that was done, she called Andrew and invited him over. She would do this official rejection on her territory as soon as he arrived.

Across town, Kurt had called Sherry into his office to have a heart to heart talk as well.

"I have the account reports you wanted" Sherry said as she walked into what she thought was a business meeting."

"Thanks, but I need to talk to you about personal stuff."

Kurt cringed when he saw the hope in her face. He hadn't liked the way he sent her away yesterday, but it couldn't be helped. It had taken a long time to see that Sherry was intentionally causing trouble in his life. But he understood that she was acting out of desperation. Something he was familiar with. He didn't want to lose Chloe even though technically he didn't have her yet. He also didn't want to lose Sherry as an employee, but he was willing to take that chance.

"I think you know how valuable you've been to me both professionally and personally."

She smiled hesitantly.

"I've decided to make some changes in my life and you have a role, if you want it."

Her smile became more assured.

"However, the role is strictly professional." He watched the smile disappear.

"I've always been grateful to you and your family for taking care of me and Meghan, but there isn't going to be anything more between us."

Sherry finally found her voice. "But I've loved you for so long. You truly never had any feelings for me? Or did they change because of Chloe?"

"I'm sorry, Sherry. But I've always looked at you as a sister."

Sherry snorted. "And Chloe?"

"I hope to marry her."

Her lips thinned. "I see. So this role for me in your life is basically keeping the job I already have?"

"Actually, I was thinking of a promotion, but I will not tolerate any more interference in my personal life."

"Can I think about it?"

"You have until tomorrow at five."

"Are you so sure that Chloe will have you? I hear Andrew is pursuing her quite intensely."

He refused to believe Chloe would choose Andrew over him, but he supposed anything was possible. "Yes, I believe she will have me."

Sherry stood. "Well, I will give you my answer by five tomorrow."

"Don't you want to know what the promotion is?"

"We'll discuss it then."

She turned to walk out and Kurt had a sinking feeling.

A business call came in and prevented him from dwelling on what just happened.

Further away, Andrew arrived at Chloe's promptly at six o'clock. He carried a bouquet of flowers similar to the ones that he had previously sent.

Chloe greeted him and accepted the flowers as well as a kiss on the cheek and then led Andrew into the living room.

Once they were both seated, Chloe jumped right in.

Taking a deep breath, she said, "Thanks for coming Andrew. Something has come to my attention and I was just wondering...when were you going to tell me you can't have children?"

The purple shade that appeared on his face was enough for her to know he had nothing more to say to her. If they had pursued their original marriage plans, he probably would wait until they became married before telling her, or possibly never intended to share it with her.

"Uh, um, who told you that?"

"Doesn't matter, is it true?"

His mouth worked with nothing coming out. Finally, his shoulders slumped. "Yes."

Chloe nodded. "Did you know this before our original marriage plans?"

Andrew leaned forward, looking at the floor. "No, it was only recently."

"And you loved me so much, that you were going to withhold this information if we pursued the marriage again?"

"Well..."

She chuckled. "Well Andrew, I'm very sorry to hear this and at least you can relate to my loss more sincerely. The bottom line now is that I have started the adoption process as a single parent. I have invited you here to officially ask you to stay out of my life. I don't need you, or anyone."

"Not even Kurt?"

She smiled. "Not even Kurt. However, I'm seriously thinking of letting him into my life and that of the child I will eventually have."

"Sherry may have something to say about that."

She shrugged. "That will be her problem." The words came out more confident than she felt.

Andrew stood. "I guess I'll go then. I truly am sorry for everything, Chloe."

"Me too, Andrew. Me too."

She sent him on his way and wished him gook luck with his life. A weight was lifted from her heart as she finally closed that chapter of her life. It was an ending she could live with. As angry as she was at Andrew for his deception, she couldn't bring herself to his level by being cruel. Her therapist would be proud.

Sending another grateful prayer to God, she finally felt she was continuing getting beyond her struggles with Him.

Now she had to deal with Kurt. The adoption process could take months or years because she chose to adopt domestically. It was time for her to truly test the waters with Kurt. She was a little giddy as she thought about the possibility of him in her life. But she knew in her heart of hearts it would be all or nothing with him.

The next day she spent in the business office. It was rare for her to do so because she worked so much from home, but she wanted to be where she didn't have to be concerned about emotional issues. She wanted to be around others who did the same work she did and only have to concentrate on inanimate objects. Then she would go to the paint store and start getting ideas on how to decorate her child's room. Her child. It was beginning to feel very real now.

Several hours later she arrived home to find a message from Kurt, asking her to meet him and Meghan at the park the next day. She laughed when he said he had left a message on her cell phone as well. Why she ever got one she'd never know.

She returned his call and left a message for him that she'd be there.

After calling Patti and her Mom to share what happened with Andrew, she did a little more computer work and then went to bed beyond exhaustion.

The dream she had included a man and children at a park, having a fun time. She assumed it was because she was going to see Kurt and most likely Meghan too.

While driving to the park, she had decided to let him into her life. His daughter was already in her heart as well. She truly was like her own. But would he really accept another child into his life? Maybe Meghan was supposed to be the only child in her life.

It was a beautiful day with barely a cloud in the sky and a nice light breeze. Since she purposefully arrived at the park earlier than she was expected, she headed for the swings. She was swinging quite high when Kurt and Meghan called to her. She slowed down and jumped off.

"Come on, Chloe, we have something to show you." Meghan took one hand and Kurt took the other one. They headed for the enclosed building used for special events. Chloe couldn't imagine what they were up to.

When they got to the entrance, Meghan told her to close her eyes. She did so reluctantly and let Kurt lead her in.

"Open your eyes," he whispered to her.

She gasped as she looked at the small room that was decorated with blue and pink ribbons, a small cake and several baskets of toys and other things for children up to the age of eight.

"Oh my."

"Come sit down." Meghan led her to a chair.

She and Kurt disappeared behind a partition set in the corner. She could hear them whispering and suddenly felt very nervous. What else were they up to?

"Okay, Chloe." Meghan yelled. "We're coming out."

Chloe gasped as father and daughter came walking toward her with white balloons and a silver tray with a small black box set in the middle. The fact that they were dressed in jeans didn't make any difference.

They stopped in front of her and both dropped to their knees. Kurt handed her the box and they both said, "Will you marry us, Chloe?"

Chloe's heart tripped and then beat so fast she thought she was going to faint. "Oh, my," she said.

Meghan giggled. "Well?"

Kurt was watching her intently, not saying a word.

Chloe smiled and wouldn't torture herself as usual, but go with her very true first response, "Yes, I will marry you... both."

"Yay," Meghan yelled and jumped into Chloe's lap. "You want to see all the presents we got for the new baby?" She jumped off and tried to pull Chloe to the table.

"In just a minute, honey."

She got up and walked into Kurt's arms and her world tilted right for a change. "Are you sure about this? I don't even know if you want another child. It's not too late for me to stop the process. Meghan is enough for me."

Kurt kissed her. "I would love to have another child, especially with you."

"But..."

"No buts, Chloe. A child is a child, no matter where it comes from."

"I do love you, Kurt Simpson."

"And I love you, Chloe Simpson to be."

"Hey, me too," Meghan said as she put her arms around both as best she could.

Chapter 11

Before the wedding date was set, both Kurt and Chloe had to separate for a short time. Kurt and Meghan helped Kurt's parents get settled in Florida and Chloe headed to California to visit her parents. It was the first trip she had taken since her recovery and when her parents had come out to her place and helped take care of her after the accident.

Even though her parents wanted to pick her up at the airport, she decided to rent a car. She still needed to be in control of things.

Greeting her parents brought tears to her eyes as she hugged them both and didn't want to let go.

"Okay baby, you can let go anytime now," her Dad said as he squeezed her tightly and laughed amidst his own tears.

Her mother was the same. "Oh, it's so good to see you, Chloe. You look wonderful."

"I miss you guys so much, especially with everything that's been going on lately."

"Well, come on in and let's get you settled." Her Dad grabbed her luggage while she and her Mom walked arm and arm into the house."

"How was your flight?" she asked.

"Uneventful, thank God. Very smooth, not like the last one I took out here years ago."

Her mother led her to the guest bedroom and the bags were thrown on the bed to be unpacked later.

"Lunch is ready," her Dad called.

They all met on the deck and sat down to a great lunch on a beautiful day.

Her Mom smiled so lovingly. "So, tell us truly how you've been feeling, especially with the adoption plans and the new man in your life."

"Well, I've put the application in and it's been accepted. Now it's just a matter of time before a child will be available, anywhere from six months to a year or longer. Unfortunately there are more children in this country available for adoption then there has been in the past, but it will still take awhile. If it doesn't work, then I'll look into foreign options just like friends have done."

Her Dad was looking at her with such love and pride that she almost started crying tears of joy.

He asked, "So, did you apply for a girl or boy, or whatever comes available?"

"Whatever becomes available, a boy would be nice since Meghan is already in my new family." She smiled so wide that both her parents laughed.

Her mother had tears in her eyes as she said, "Honey… we can't tell you how proud we are of your recovery and the blessings that you have received since that nightmare of an accident and unfortunately the Andrew situation."

Her father cleared his throat and her mother just looked at him. "I'm sorry Jim, but I'm just so glad that she's moved on from him and found someone worthwhile. Meghan sounds like an angel too."

"She is, even though she's a challenge at times. But then, that's normal for an eight year old, right?"

Both her parents rolled their eyes and the rest of the lunch was spent talking about Chloe, Sandy and brother Peter at that age.

Her Dad started cleaning up the table and left Chloe and her mother to speak alone.

"You look great, Chloe, but a little tired. Maybe you should lie down for awhile."

"It's just from the flight, Mom, don't worry. I do tend to show tiredness a little more often these days, but it's getting better as time goes on. Plus, the flight was pretty early."

"Tell me more about Kurt. You're sure he's the one?"

"Yes, I am. Do you doubt it?"

"Well, it's not so much doubt as it is concern that he deserves you. After all, you thought Andrew was the right one too."

"I know, Mom, and I truly believed that he was the one. I'd hate to think the accident was a good thing to prevent me from making a mistake by marrying him, but I'm not so sure things wouldn't have worked out if we got married and couldn't have had kids because of his situation. It's just something we'll never know."

"And you believe that Kurt sincerely loves you and doesn't just want you to be a mother to his daughter?"

"Gee, Mom, that's a bit crude."

"Listen, Chloe, we almost lost you once and we don't want to do so again because of different circumstances."

Chloe did not expect this from her mother. Obviously her parents had kept these concerns to themselves until they saw her in person.

"Mom…"

Her mother lifted her hand. "I know you weren't expecting this, dear, but we just want to be sure you don't have any setbacks since you've come so far."

Her Dad came back out to join them. "Honey, we want what is best for you. You've been through too much to not get what you deserve."

Chloe looked at both of them. "I appreciate your concern, but I do love him and he loves me. I have no doubts about it anymore. Plus, I truly believe that God has been guiding me to this new life in spite of the struggles I've had with Him regarding me not being able to have a baby."

Her Mom and Dad smiled and then her Mom took her hand.

"Okay, then we will support the wedding. We both believe that God has truly taken care of you in spite of your struggles. We are still very sorry you can't have a child, but we are beyond grateful that you are still alive."

Her father took her other hand and kissed it and asked another question.

"And you're sure he's open to adoption?"

"Most definitely Dad. In fact, he's the one who kept telling me he wanted to be a part of it, even though I said I was willing to stop it since his daughter would be in my life. Even though I applied as a single parent, they have all the background information on him as well because of the upcoming wedding.

Chloe's Dad actually looked teary eyed. "You deserve this honey and we just want to protect you any way we can."

"Thanks Mom and Dad. I love you guys. And by the way, he's going to sell his house and move into mine."

Her Mom raised her eyebrows. "Really? I thought he'd want the daughter to be where her mother had been."

"Me too," her Dad said.

Chloe sighed. "I thought the same thing, but he feels that it's time to truly move on and try something new. There will be plenty of things that will be reminders to Meghan of her Mom. Unfortunately, she has been forgetting things already. He shows her pictures now and then to help her remember."

"Have you planned when the wedding and the move will be?"

"Not yet, but I want to know what your schedule looks like in the next few months so you can come out for the wedding."

Her Mom and Dad glanced at each other and he nodded to her Mom.

"What's going on you guys?"

Her Dad reached for the Mom's hand and they both looked at her with huge smiles on their faces.

"Well, honey," her Mom started. "Even though we really like being out here in California for all the years we have been, we really enjoyed being on the east coast taking care of you. Of course, the reason wasn't a good one, but it just brought back a lot of memories from the years we grew up there, met and even had you kids."

Chloe's heart started racing.

She looked at her husband again. "We've been thinking of possibly moving back there."

"Really?"

Her Dad leaned forward. "Yes honey. Since my business can be run from anywhere I'm located at, when we went to take care of you, I looked into options for the business. The bottom line is, we should be closer to you kids, especially after that accident."

Chloe's head went in so many different directions with the thoughts of them being close to potential new grandchildren that were so encouraging.

As important as it is for people to live their lives wherever they want, especially how good communication is now these days, this would be a great idea.

"Oh my God you guys. That would be great, especially for when I get children in my life. Sandy and Peter would love it too."

Her Dad smiled. "You are the first one we've mentioned it too, honey."

******

Across the country in Florida, Kurt's parents were grilling him as well. His wife's parents were also in the area and Meghan was spending the day with them.

He had talked to his parents about Chloe when he realized he had fallen for her and wanted her in their lives. With the move to Florida happening, there wasn't enough time to really focus on things once he told them he asked her to marry him.

"Listen you guys, I love her. Meghan loves her and she loves both of us. Hopefully we'll have more kids through adoption."

His mother and father looked at each other and then his father spoke. "We just want to be sure this is what you want, son. You've been through a lot raising Meghan yourself and your mother and I, not to mention your brothers, just want to be sure."

"I appreciate your concern. The truth is, I almost blew it with Chloe because of some things involving Sherry. I never knew Sherry had her eye on me for more than friendship."

"Well," his mother responded. "We always knew Sherry had plans for you. Her mother always told me so. In fact, I spoke to her the other day and she said that Sherry was quite upset over the whole thing."

"Well, I'm sorry about Sherry, especially since she decided to leave my company, but I had always looked at her as a sister. Meghan is my priority and as you've heard her talk about Chloe, you should be convinced that it's good for all of us."

"What about the adoption? She's doing it herself?"

"She went through a bad time with her ex and even though we'll be married, the process was started as a single parent. The powers that be have all the investigation information on me now."

"And, I want you to know that I will be selling my place and moving into hers."

His Mom and Dad looked at each other.

"Okay, Kurt," his mother said. "We wondered what your decision would be. Obviously, Chloe may have felt uncomfortable being in your home permanently. We'll definitely support you on this. As important as memories are about your wife, it's also important for you to live your new life in a new place. Your brothers will be here shortly and have their own grilling to do."

Both parents laughed as Kurt rolled his eyes. Thirty minutes later his younger brothers arrived and tackled him, pinning him to the ground and grilling him while their parents watched and laughed.

He was able to get estimated times when they could make it up for the wedding. His brothers were staying with them a little longer before heading back up to Connecticut.

The next morning, Chloe and Kurt communicated and shared each other's family interrogations. They laughed at first, but then got serious. Both had actually thought of everything that their families had brought up and knew that what they had was real. They were determined not to let normal doubts stop their plans. It was agreed that any serious doubts had to be communicated so they didn't get out of control.

When they arrived back in Connecticut a few days later, plans began to sell Kurt's house and start the process to move into Chloe's. When they saw each other after being away, they knew it was truly meant for them to be together.

They took Meghan to pick out what kind of paint or wallpaper she wanted for her new room, as well as ideas for the new child that would eventually come.

When they were looking at the wallpaper, Meghan took her father away from Chloe. "Dad, do you think Mom would be upset that we're moving and you're getting married again?"

Kurt was caught off guard, especially since they had already spoken about this, but bent to be more at her level. "No, honey, I think Mommy would be glad that we're living our lives, especially with someone like Chloe. But we already talked about this, right?"

"Yeah, but I heard Mommy's parents talking about it and I think they were disappointed that you were getting married again."

Kurt remembered having the conversation with them as well. "Oh honey, I think they meant that it was too bad for me because their daughter was no longer here and I had to move on. Not that they don't want me to re-marry." He looked up and saw Chloe on the other side of the wallpaper samples. She had a sad smile on her face, but understanding as well.

"Oh, okay. I love Grammy and Papa and I don't want them to be sad anymore."

"I think they are happy for both of us, honey."

"Are they coming to the wedding?"

"No, they aren't able to make it, but they did say they'd be sending us a present."

"Us?"

"Yep."

"Oh, goody. I wonder what it is?"

"We'll see in time. Have you decided what you want for the bedroom?"

"Yes. Where's Chloe?"

"She's over there looking at paint samples."

Father and daughter walked hand and hand to where Chloe was standing.

After making the choices to do the bedroom, they decided to go to the Chinese restaurant and Meghan was excellent using the chopsticks. Chloe's boss and his wife were there again as well and stopped by to congratulate them on their plans. Chloe was still going to do the computer work for them.

During dessert they talked about going to church together on Sunday. Chloe was still a little hesitant even though she was grateful for the new life in her future. At least she still had one and this was most likely the more positive chance to enter the church.

They were also going to set up a meeting with the Pastor to discuss the wedding plans.

Chloe was looking forward to talking to her psychologist, especially since it had been several weeks since she last saw her.

After the dinner, Kurt and Meghan went back to their home to start getting stuff together and Chloe went to hers. She decided to meet them at the church instead of going together. As much as she was looking to sincerely go into the church, she still didn't want to remove an option for her to change her mind if necessary.

Once she organized more things in her place, she went on the computer and then hit the sack.

In the middle of the night she woke up screaming and felt sick to her stomach. It took several seconds before she remembered the dream. It was similar to the car accident, but the baby she usually dreamed of disappeared as the accident happened.

After taking several deep breaths and shedding a few tears, a relief over took her. She laid back down and finally understood. In past dreams she reached for a baby that was always in reach but could never be touched. Now the dream had the baby disappear because that's what the injury was going to do to her. The reality was that the child would not exist, at least not as one out of her body.

Thoughts of Meghan made her smile and true love for Kurt brought happy tears. She was finally able to feel comforted and fell back to sleep.

The next morning she drove to church and saw Kurt and Meghan talking to the priest on the stairs.

They turned to see Chloe climbing the steps and it was obvious that Kurt was concerned if she'd make it through the doors.

She shook hands with the priest and then took Meghan's hand as the three of them entered the church together.

Goosebumps went through Chloe as she walked down the aisle to the pew they chose. Once she entered the pew and kneeled, tears lurked in her eyes, but didn't fall. She felt so comforted and forgiven by God that she just wanted to hug Meghan and Kurt forever.

Sitting with them felt so real, as if they had been doing this routine for a long time.

Once the mass was over, Kurt explained the time options to meet with the priest.

They went to a local restaurant for breakfast and discussed more about the wedding.

Since it was a second one for him and a first for her, they both agreed to have a regular church ceremony.

Kurt's neighbors were at the restaurant and asked for Meghan to join them.

Once she joined them, Chloe reached across the table and took his hands in hers.

"Thank you, Kurt, for being in my life and accepting me as I am without the chance to have a child that is truly yours and mine physically."

Kurt squeezed her hands. "I love you, Chloe, and just being blessed with you in my life and Meghan's is more than I could ever dream of."

Chloe squeezed his hands back. "God has truly guided us honey, in spite of the pain of losses and dealing with them. He brought us together as a true gift to us after our losses. Unfortunately loss can help see life more sincerely and challenge us to live it better and in honor of our Lord."

Kurt lifted her hand and kissed it. "Life is always a challenge, regardless of situations. It's just nice to have more positive, happy times than losses and painful times."

"I agree Kurt. God does look out for us and helps us to deal with sad things and enjoy happy things. It makes me feel guilty about how angry I was with him.

"I understand how you feel, but I'm sure He understands how humans are supposed to feel. Then He has the patience for us to come back to Him and live life truly as He wants us to."

They finished the meal and each headed to their own places again.

The next few weeks were spent moving Kurt and Meghan into Chloe's home. Part of her was looking forward to it and also wondering how it was going to be with others in her place on a daily basis, especially after so many years on her own, even while in the relationship with Andrew.

The bedrooms were set up first so there would be options on where they would stay while getting their home ready to sell.

Once everything was moved into Chloe's, a wedding date was set after meeting with the priest a few times.

The wedding was going to be in September, two weekends after Labor Day.

They opted to make their honeymoon plans a family trip to Disneyworld in Florida and then Disneyland in California. It was more important to spend the time as a family than just a couple. In the near future they would take their honeymoon time to be alone together.

Once Meghan's bedroom was all set, Chloe took her out for lunch so they could have one on one time.

"Meghan, can I ask you a question?"

"Sure"

"Are you looking forward to being an older sister?"

Meghan laughed. "I don't think I have any choice."

Chloe smiled. "Well, I wanted to tell you that you are to truly be a special older sister. Everyone has moody times, but you are a great daughter. And I'm not just saying that honey, I truly believe it."

Meghan smiled. "And are you ready to be a Mommy to me and possibly others?"

Chloe was thrown off by those questions. She smiled. "Well, I guess time will tell, right?"

Meghan laughed and shrugged.

Chloe reached over and took a hand. "I love you very much, honey, and I know I won't replace your mother at all, but I will love and care for you for all of your life. And I know that anyone else that comes into this family will be truly loved and cared for by me and your father, along with you, big sister." She smiled and squeezed her hand.

"Chloe, I truly love you too. Still sorry I can't remember a lot about my Mom, but appreciate Dad's pictures and stories. I appreciate your respect for her. Sorry you never knew her."

"Well, honey, I have a feeling your Mom's spirit is here with us and she's smiling."

The two finished their meal and had dessert and headed back home. *Home.*

Chloe hid her smile while thinking they were going home. Silent thank you prayers were sent to God for filling in her life with what she thought was taken from her.

When they arrived at home and went inside, Meghan ran to her father and said, "Hi Dad, I'm soon to be an older sister."

He glanced at Chloe and smiled. "That is quite true honey. How do you feel about that?"

"I'm looking forward to it Dad. I know that you and Chloe will love us all."

They hugged each other and then Meghan went to her room.

Kurt walked over to Chloe and kissed and hugged her.

"How was the meal?"

"It was good and nice to be one on one with her at a restaurant. I truly wanted to know how she felt about all these changes."

"And, she wanted to know if I was ready to be a Mommy to her and possibly others."

Kurt tilted his head. "Really? Did it throw you off a bit?"

Chloe laughed, "Yes it did, but the conversation was good and encouraging."

Kurt kissed and hugged her again. "You are going to make a great mother, honey. I've no doubts about it."

Chloe kissed and hugged him back. "Just like the great daddy you will be to the new one too."

"One?"

Chloe slapped his arm. "At least one at a time."

They both laughed and then continued to organize stuff in her house.

Once they were all settled in Chloe's house, it felt more and more like it was truly meant to be.

Chloe's physical therapy appointments were finally completed and she went to see her psychologist a few weeks before the wedding. She would see her again in three months and then eventually will stop the appointments.

Chloe's parents came and stayed with their son and were looking for a new place in the Connecticut area while waiting for the wedding. Her sister and brother were so happy to hear they were moving back to the east coast.

Kurt's parents did come after saying they wouldn't and stayed at a local hotel and met up with Chloe's family.

Chloe and Kurt's out of town relatives came in the week before the wedding.

Both Chloe and Kurt felt as if they had been with all these people for a very long time. It was another confirmation that it was meant for them to be together.

The day of the wedding was an awesome weather day. It was a little warm, but not too muggy for that time of year. Meghan was the maid of honor and Chloe's sister and her friend Patti and Kurt's brothers, along with Chloe's were the rest of the wedding party.

Walking down the aisle, Chloe spoke to God from her heart and soul. Appreciated him forgiving her and blessing her, along with Kurt and Meghan.

The ceremony was awesome and she was so amazed at how many friends and family were there.

As they kissed when the priest announced them husband and wife, Meghan walked up and put her arms around both.

"I love you Mommy and Daddy."

Chloe and Kurt looked at each other and then Kurt picked up his daughter and he and Chloe hugged her. Everyone in the church clapped and cheered for them. Their parents nodded at each other and raised their thumbs.

After the mass was complete, they went to the park for the reception. All the children were able to play outside and families had plenty of time to finish getting to know each other.

The next day, they left for the Disney trips and returned home two weeks later.

While they were away, Kurt received two offers for his house.

They waited until they returned before accepting one offer. They also planned to have their own honeymoon trip down the road once everything was settled. Her sister would take care of Meghan.

Six months into their new life the call came and 8th month old Jamie was to join their family. Meghan was excited to have a baby brother. Since babies were very rare for domestic adoptions, the Simpson's felt very blessed. They also felt they could take on another child. A year later, two year old Maggie arrived, completing the family that Chloe had always hoped for.

THE END